His lips touched her cheek...

A feeling of guilt swept over her. How could she think of kissing another man after she'd been talking about David?

'David was hailed as a hero. He won a posthumous award for bravery. The girls are so proud of their hero father.'

'Quite something to live up to,' he said evenly.

'They certainly think so.'

'And so do you, Jackie.'

Margaret Barker pursued a variety of interesting careers before she became a full-time author. Besides holding a BA degree in French and Linguistics, she is a Licentiate of the Royal Academy of Music, a State Registered Nurse and a qualified teacher. Happily married, she has two sons, a daughter, and an increasing number of grandchildren. She lives with her husband in a sixteenth-century thatched house near the East Anglian coast.

Recent titles by the same author:

HOME-COMING
I'D LOVE A BABY!
INTIMATE PRESCRIPTION

HERO'S LEGACY

BY
MARGARET BARKER

MILLS & BOON®

First published in Great Britain 1998
Harlequin Mills & Boon Limited,
Eton House, 18-24 Paradise Road, Richmond, Surrey TW9 1SR

© Margaret Barker 1998

ISBN 0 263 15756 3

Set in Times Roman 10 on 11½ pt.
15-9805-53589-D

Printed and bound in Great Britain
by Antony Rowe Ltd, Chippenham, Wiltshire

CHAPTER ONE

JACKIE drove into the surgery car park and slammed on her brakes. Someone had pinched her parking space and one glance at that sleek, steel-grey, expensive car told her who the culprit was.

She remembered looking out of her surgery window when she was interviewing Tom Prestwick for the vacancy in her practice and temporarily losing her train of thought. She wondered now, as she had done on that interview day, if her new partner had any idea what the muddy country lanes around here could do to a beautiful car like that! This was his first day, but he'd soon find out when he went out on house calls.

She parked in Dr Vickers's old space, wondering fleetingly how her ex-partner was enjoying life in London. He'd never been cut out for a country practice and it had been a relief when he'd said he was leaving.

There had been numerous applications for the vacancy and she remembered how difficult it had been to draw up a short-list. But, after much soul-searching and consultation with Meg Gresham, her partner, Tom Prestwick had been chosen.

As she hurried in through the back door of the surgery she couldn't help wishing she'd managed to arrive before the new doctor. As senior partner, she should have been there to welcome him and show him the ropes, but no doubt Helen, her capable receptionist, would have the situation under control.

'Good morning, Helen. I see Dr Prestwick's arrived before me.'

Helen Morgan paused in her work of feeding medical information into the central computer.

'He's waiting in your consulting room, Jackie. Shall I bring some coffee? You look as if you need some. Have you had a rush to get here?'

Jackie sank down onto the nearest chair and gave her a rueful smile.

'No more than usual. The twins had forgotten to get their cookery ingredients ready so there was a lot of rushing around in the kitchen early this morning as they weighed out flour and sugar and all the rest of it. Fiona dropped a carton of eggs so Debbie said she would scramble them for breakfast. It was her turn to cook and it seemed like a good idea at the time, except it took longer than she thought and they nearly missed the school bus.'

'I'm not surprised! My three never cooked breakfast when they were still at school.'

Jackie leaned back against the chair. 'It was something we started soon after...when we were first on our own. I thought it would be a good start to the day. We were all in a state of shock and I wanted to feel that we were still a family.'

She took a deep breath as she tried to push away the feelings of sadness which were threatening to sweep over her.

'Debbie and Fiona have been brilliant about it, always taking their turn in the kitchen. When they were eleven their first efforts were sometimes pretty disastrous, but now that they're sixteen I really look forward to our little family meals. You know, Helen, the girls have been such a comfort to me since...'

Her voice trailed away. She ought to get on with some work instead of indulging in a heart to heart. But Helen had this effect on her. She'd been Jackie's father's medical secretary for years and she'd been a constant source of comfort in the days when Jackie had needed it most.

Helen reached out and patted Jackie's hand. 'I think

you've coped brilliantly. It's a good thing you're still young enough to look after your family *and* run the practice.'

Jackie smiled. 'Not all that young! I'm thirty-five next month, Helen.'

'That's young, believe me!'

Helen put her head on one side, as if scrutinising her. 'But time goes so quickly. You know, Jackie, you ought to get out more, have some fun. It would do you good.'

'Oh, we have a lot of fun at home,' Jackie said quickly. 'I don't see why I should force myself to go out if I don't want to.'

She stood up. 'I'd better go and see the new doctor. Have you got his file, Helen? I'd like to refresh my memory.'

Helen was delving into the filing cabinet. 'I'll get it for you. It'll be good for you to have another doctor to help you. Since Dr Vickers left you've been rushed off your feet, and what with Meg taking four weeks' holiday, I'm not surprised everything's getting on top of you and—'

'Everything's not getting on top of me, Helen. I simply—'

'Well, let's just say you've been on a bit of a short fuse lately, and I don't blame you with everything you've got on your plate... Ah, here it is. Dr Tom Prestwick.'

Helen smiled as she handed over the envelope.

'Thanks, Helen.' Jackie pulled out a sheaf of papers and studied the first page.

'Tom Prestwick, age 39.' She turned to look at Helen.

'He was a senior registrar, in line for a consultancy post, when he decided to go into general practice, you know. He did his GP training with an inner London group practice and he's got glowing references both from the hospital and from the practice. I was very impressed when I interviewed him. He seemed to stand out from the others. And he was perfectly happy to be a salaried partner for the first year, with an option to buy in after that.'

Helen nodded. 'Your father always insisted on that arrangement. Very wise, I think.'

Jackie glanced up at Helen. 'One thing intrigues me. Why would a man in line for a consultancy want to bury himself in the backwoods of Essex?'

Helen shrugged. 'Search me. Why don't you go and ask him?'

Jackie gave a mischievous grin. 'Perhaps I will. I'll march in there and say, 'Hey, Dr Prestwick, don't you realise you're going to die of boredom out here?'.'

Helen laughed. For a moment she'd glimpsed the young Jackie she'd known when she'd first started working for her father. She'd been so full of fun and vitality before her world had crashed in on her.

'Dr Prestwick is probably dying of boredom while he's waiting for you up there.'

'In that case, I'd better go and start mouth-to-mouth resuscitation.' Jackie smiled. 'On second thoughts, perhaps not! Would you be an angel and bring some coffee soon, Helen? That would definitely help.'

As Jackie stood up and crossed the tiled floor towards the stairs that led to her room, she could smell the disinfectant which the cleaner had dispensed liberally with her squeezy mop. That distinctive smell always signalled the start of her professional day. Making her way up the stairs, she reflected that it was a good thing she loved her work as a country doctor.

Her professional life was very important to her and immensely satisfying. She found she gained strength from helping her patients. And for the past five years she'd needed to be strong.

At the top of the stairs she paused and glanced at the round, antique, brass-framed mirror that hung on the pastel-painted wall. She remembered that mirror so well from her childhood here in the surgery house. Her grandfather had picked her up and held her in his arms as she'd looked into it, and the reflection she'd seen had never ceased to amaze her.

It amazed her now, all right! Dark, wispy strands of hair had escaped from their imprisonment within the severe, serviceable chignon she'd hastily arranged at her nape. She ran her hands over the sides of her head and swept the offending strands backwards. That was better! The dab of lipstick she'd applied at the crack of dawn had completely disappeared. If she got a break between patients she'd do something about that.

Not that anyone would notice! But there was something about the application of lipstick that made her feel she wasn't entirely out of touch with the world of glamour. Possibly it was an errant feeling from her youth when she'd taken an enormous amount of time getting ready to go out, even if she'd only been going to post a letter.

She peered more closely. Yes, there were definitely a couple of grey hairs near her temple. She could tweak them out or let the patients see how old and wise she was. Probably the latter!

She pushed open the door.

'Good morning, Dr Prestwick,' she said to the distinguished-looking man, sitting beside her desk. 'Sorry to keep you waiting. Family commitments, you know...or probably you don't know.'

She reached her desk and stopped babbling. It was her normal reaction to unknown men nowadays. She realised she was completely out of touch with the opposite sex. Oh, she was OK with patients. More than OK, in fact.

In a professional situation she had the sex difference completely under control. Just the right amount of firmness, if a male patient seemed to be overstepping the mark, would bring him back into line.

But in new encounters with unknown men she hid behind

a stream of words to cover her embarrassment. As she sat down behind her desk she looked across at the new member of her medical team and decided that she liked what she saw. Yes, she'd definitely made the right choice.

Tom Prestwick's hair was mid-brown with a hint of auburn and possibly a few strands of grey around the ears, but she could be mistaken. She'd have to lean closer to get a better look and that would be totally unprofessional.

He had a nice face, she decided. In fact, it was more than nice—dared she admit that she found him handsome? He had strong, high cheek-bones and dark, distinctive eyebrows over his brown eyes. Were they brown or hazel? They certainly had a touch of hazel.

He looked very smart, just as he had for the interview—a well-cut grey suit, immaculately ironed, and a white shirt teamed with a discreet, blue striped tie.

She experienced a momentary feeling of apprehension as he placed both hands on her desk, facing her with an air of lightly veiled impatience. One of the dark, distinctive eyebrows was raised slightly.

'I arrived early, Dr Brent, so that I could get organised before the patients arrived.'

She bridled at the hint of a reprimand in his deep, gravelly voice.

'Oh, I don't expect you to see any patients on your first day, Dr Prestwick,' she said firmly, folding her hands on the desk as she looked across at him, her face composed into her 'senior partner' expression.

'Today you can look around the surgery, ask any questions you need answering, discover the intricacies and delights of the new computer system, find out what we can and can't do in the treatment room and so on.'

The door opened and Helen came in with a tray, complete with an ornate coffee-pot, sugar, milk and two cups and saucers.

Jackie raised her eyebrows as she recognised the crockery from her father's era—usually reserved for important visitors.

'Quite a change from the usual mugs, Helen.'

Helen smiled as she put the tray down on Jackie's desk and picked up the china coffee-pot.

'Don't give the game away, Dr Brent. I thought Dr Prestwick should have the VIP treatment on his first day.'

Jackie noticed how her receptionist was positively simpering in front of the new doctor. Glancing across at Tom Prestwick, she saw that he, too, was now radiating charm as he accepted the coffee that Helen had poured out.

'Thank you... And your name is...?'

'Oh, just call me Helen.'

Jackie was fascinated to see the way Helen ran both hands over her greying blonde hair, before smoothing the sides of her black and white check pleated skirt over her ample hips.

'And what exactly do you do here, Helen, besides make excellent coffee?'

Tom Prestwick took an appreciative sip, before leaning back against the wooden chair that suddenly seemed too small to accommodate his long, wiry body.

Helen was now leaning against the door, as if reluctant to leave, obviously hoping for a long chat with the intriguing new doctor.

'Oh, I'm part of the fixtures and fittings around here, Dr Prestwick. I do everything except cure the patients. Twenty years ago when I first started it was all so different. Just Jackie's dad and me. Then suddenly new houses started sprouting up in the fields around here and we had to expand. Three doctors we need nowadays and a part-time nursing sister for the treatment room.'

'Meg Gresham, our second doctor—you met her when you came for your interview—is on holiday at the moment,'

Jackie explained. 'And our third doctor took a hospital post in London a couple of months ago, which was when we advertised the post.'

'Dr Vickers said he couldn't stand living out here in the back of beyond,' Helen said. 'There isn't much goes on in Benton village. I hope you won't regret moving out from the bright lights, Dr Prestwick.'

He put his coffee-cup down on the desk and adjusted the stiff white cuffs peeping from the sleeves of his jacket. 'I'm sure I won't. I needed a change from London.'

Jackie heard the edge in his voice and had the distinct impression there was a compelling reason for his move out here. She watched as he stretched his long legs and stood up.

Helen darted forward. 'Another coffee, Doctor?'

He smiled and shook his head. 'No, thanks. If someone could show me the room I'll be using I'll get myself organised.'

'Is Dr Vickers's room ready, Helen?' Jackie asked, praying that she would get an affirmative answer.

'Of course it is. I spent ages sorting out all those old, dog-eared medical magazines that had been gathering dust. And Dot came in and gave it a good clean this morning.'

Tom Prestwick turned as he reached the door. 'I'm available if you need an extra pair of hands today, Dr Brent.'

'Unless there's a real emergency I won't need you, Dr Prestwick,' Jackie said.

Helen was holding open the door, an ingratiating smile on her face. Jackie, watching as her new partner went out, decided he would be a definite asset to the practice with his tall, distinguished good looks, excellent qualifications and wealth of experience. He exuded confidence. The patients would feel very safe in his hands and she would have no qualms about his medical capabilities.

She'd never really taken to Alan Vickers in the two years he'd been with the practice. And he hadn't pulled his weight—always asking for time off to go up to London to see his friends. No, she was better off without him.

She rubbed a hand over the knot of tension at the back of her neck, stood up and walked over to the window. Her room looked out over the garden at the back of the building. Although it was only the middle of May, because of the mild spring they'd enjoyed that year the lilac trees were already in full blossom.

Beyond the garden was a field, sprouting lettuces in long even rows. The farmer and a couple of agricultural labourers were raking away the weeds. At the end of the field she could see the tall fir trees that marked the boundary of her own garden.

She wondered fleetingly if Beth, her cleaning lady, had arrived yet, and if she'd seen the note about the wonky shower unit. Bill Turner, the plumber, had promised to come in during the couple of hours that Beth would be there this morning, but his sense of timing wasn't all that brilliant.

The intercom buzzed. 'Your first patient is here, Dr Brent. Shall I send her up?'

Jackie smiled as she heard Helen using her posh, professional voice.

'Yes, please, Mrs Morgan,' she returned, knowing that Helen was always amused to get her full title.

Her first patient, Lorraine Dewhirst, was expecting her first baby in August and was very nervous. As she waddled into the surgery Jackie could immediately see that she was carrying too much weight. After the preliminary chat about the weather and how she was feeling, subjects of conversation designed to relax her patient, Jackie suggested that Lorraine step onto the scales.

Lorraine frowned and stayed put on her seat. 'They

weighed me at the hospital last month. I was a bit over, but not too much so I don't think you need to worry about me.'

'All the same, I think it would be a good idea if—'

'My mum says I need all the food I can get. I'm eating for two, you know,' she said in a defensive tone.

It never ceased to amaze Jackie that there were still women who peddled this old wives' tale to their daughters. Patiently she explained that being overweight in pregnancy could have a bad effect on both the mother and the baby.

'By all means, eat a good balanced diet but don't snack on high-calorie things like crisps, biscuits, cakes...'

'I try not to, Doctor, but my mum's always bringing me chocolates to cheer me up.' She paused. 'Maybe I'd better have a look at how much weight I've put on because I have been a bit hungry this month.'

Jackie waited by the scale as Lorraine took off her shoes. As soon as she stepped on, the pointer shot up to an alarming level.

Lorraine put a hand over her mouth in dismay. 'My God, I've put on...well...you work it out, Doctor, will you?'

'You've put on too much, Lorraine,' Jackie said quietly. 'Now come and sit down and we'll talk about it. If you're going to be fit enough to have a healthy baby you're going to have to control your appetite. I don't want to scare you but these are the facts...'

For several minutes they looked over the diet sheets and discussed why it was necessary to stick to them. After this, Jackie took Lorraine's blood pressure. It was, as Jackie had expected, too high. She explained to Lorraine that this was one of the dangerous side-effects of obesity.

'I'd like you to come and see me every week, Lorraine. We've got three months to go and if you control your weight it will ensure your baby is healthy. If you carry on eating too much you'll have to spend the last few weeks in hospital.'

'My Trevor wouldn't like that. He can't boil an egg.'

'Well, for the sake of your husband and your baby, you must stick to the diet sheet,' Jackie said, gently patting her patient's bloated, dimpled hand.

She felt very sorry for Lorraine as she watched her easing herself slowly through the door. Only twenty-one years old and already she was too firmly entrenched in the wrong pattern of eating. Probably her well-intentioned mother was to blame, but it wasn't too late to change the situation for the sake of Lorraine's and the baby's health.

She'd known Lorraine since she was a schoolgirl and, as with all the patients she'd known for a long time, she was very fond of her. It was difficult sometimes to detach herself from her patients' problems, however much she tried to be objective about her work.

She remembered how Lorraine had come to see her when she was sixteen and asked to be put on the Pill. She was in love with Trevor Dewhirst, one of the boys at school, and they were having a sexual relationship but she didn't want her mum to know. She'd said her mother was very strait-laced and old-fashioned, and wouldn't understand.

Jackie had thought long and hard about this one because Enid Backhouse was also one of her patients. She'd tried to persuade Lorraine to confide in her mum but she'd been adamant that she daren't. So, taking the line that prevention was better than a teenage pregnancy, Lorraine had been put on the Pill.

When she was seventeen Mrs Backhouse had found the Pill in her daughter's bedroom drawer and had been furious with her. Lorraine had come sobbing to the surgery, saying she wanted to leave home and asking Jackie to help her to get her a flat of her own. But after a few weeks the matter was resolved by Mrs Backhouse insisting on a white wedding in Benton village church.

After the wedding Enid Backhouse couldn't wait to hear

the pitter-patter of tiny feet and was constantly in the surgery, asking Jackie if she thought Lorraine should be checked out because nothing had happened. Now, expecting her first grandchild, she was beside herself with grandmotherly joy and was obviously lavishing the wrong kind of attention on her daughter in the form of comfort eating.

Jackie wondered if she should have a word with the formidable matriarch but shelved the idea for the moment. Enid had her own weight problem to contend with and wouldn't take any notice of her advice. No, she would just have to hope that Lorraine would see the sense of taking care of herself and the baby—but she would have to be strong to stand up to that mother of hers!

Jackie worked steadily through the list of patients. Some were friends she'd known for years and she had to spend longer with them, listening to the latest gossip or talking to the small children and babies who'd been brought along because their parents couldn't leave them at home or because they simply wanted Jackie to admire and comment on how well they were doing.

'Hasn't she grown!'

'Yes, she's going to be as tall as her brother soon.'

'Lovely hair! I remember that was the first thing I noticed when she was born...'

It was important that she took an interest in each and every one of them.

As the last patient went she leaned back in her chair and stretched her arms high above her head. She would dash home to see if the plumber had been, eat a quick sandwich and— She frowned as the door opened. Surely not another patient?

'Oh, it's you, Dr Prestwick. Can I help you?'

He remained framed in the doorway with his arms folded, leaning against the wall with an enigmatic expression on his face. For a brief second Jackie thought that he seemed un-characteristically tentative.

'Have I caught you at a bad time? You sound a bit har-assed.'

'Sorry. Do come in. I was just planning a quick getaway and I thought you might be yet another patient. What can I do for you?'

His tense features relaxed and he smiled as he walked towards her, his highly polished leather shoes moving swiftly over the carpet in front of her desk.

'It's more what I can do for you, Dr Brent. I'd like to take you out for lunch.' His smile became whimsical. 'From a medical point of view, you look as if you could do with a square meal.'

Nobody had commented on her being skinny for years! Certainly not a newly appointed recruit to the firm. What a nerve! But, still, there was something rather appealing about his smile. He meant well, and it would be a good opportunity to get to know him better.

'I've got to call in at home to see if the plumber's been. If he hasn't I'll have to hang around until—'

'That's no problem,' he said, in a decisive tone. 'Let's go and see. You don't live far away, do you?'

'No, just at the end of the lane. I bring the car down here so that it's ready for emergencies. I could equally well walk here, but you know how it is if you have to dash out to a patient's home in a hurry and...'

She was doing it again, getting flustered simply because she was alone with a man she didn't know. She was appre-hensive about men who tried to take the lead, like Tom Prestwick was doing. She was the senior partner, for heaven's sake! Let him show a little deference!

'We'll have to be back by two,' she said quickly. 'I've got the mother and baby clinic and...'

He raised one dark eyebrow. 'I thought Sister Rosemary Saunders took the clinic?'

From the look in his eyes she could swear that he was amused by something. Maybe it was because he sensed she was flapping a bit.

'Well, yes, she does. I can see you've been making yourself familiar with our surgery routine. But I have to be here in case she needs me for a difficult case.'

'I see.'

His tone was overtly thoughtful, but she could tell he'd marked her out as being over-anxious.

'I'll come down the lane and wait at your house with you, if I may, and then we can go off somewhere for lunch. I'm told there's a quaint little pub down by the harbour in Estersea. Far enough to be away from our patients and near enough to get back here if we're needed.'

She was sure she knew which quaint little pub he was referring to, and felt a pang of apprehension. She hadn't been in there since... Perhaps she should suggest somewhere else. She took a deep breath. No, it would be good for her to go in there again and try to put the poignant memories in their place.

Tom Prestwick had got everything worked out, hadn't he? she thought as they went out to the car park. It was a long time since someone had tried to organise her like this. Part of her resented it but, on the other hand, she had to admit that she found it quite relaxing to be taken care of for a change.

'Your car, I believe?' She stood at the side of the magnificent vehicle. 'This is actually my parking space. You can have the one I had to park in this morning.'

His brown eyes flickered as he looked down at her quizzically.

'Is there a problem about parking spaces?' he asked, his even tone giving nothing away.

'Well, no, but…' She hesitated. It hadn't occurred to her that he might pursue the matter. 'It's just that we've always kept to our own spaces in the past. You can see they're all numbered. I've got number one, Meg has two, so…'

He gave her a wry smile. 'So I'm number three. Making sure I keep my place as the new boy.'

'I didn't mean—'

'I'm sure you didn't. Fair enough. Look, it's not worth making an issue about.'

'I wasn't making an issue about it.'

He raised an eyebrow. 'Fine. I've said I'll toe the line. You've got your rules out here so let's stick to them.'

She drew in her breath as she recognised that underneath Tom's veneer of charm there was a strong, decisive character who would probably begin to question the firmly established workings of her beloved practice.

'My car or yours?' she asked quickly.

'Let's take mine.'

Deliberately she ignored her apprehensive feelings as she climbed into Tom Prestwick's car. It was early days so there was bound to be tension between two working colleagues initially, she told herself.

Mmm, she liked the smell of the luxurious leather seats that wafted across as she sank down into the passenger seat. What was this car, anyway? No clue on the walnut dashboard. Cars had never interested her, except as a means of transport from A to B, but she would certainly enjoy being transported in such style!

As he drove her down the little lane that led to her cottage she was thinking about the journey they would make down to Estersea after she'd been in home. She must remember to duck her head down in the seat as they passed Estersea High School. If Debbie and Fiona were out in the playground she would never hear the end of it.

'What a charming cottage!' Tom Prestwick was full of

admiration as he pulled the car into her semi-circular drive-way and brought it to a halt in front of the sturdy oak door. 'How old is it?'

'Sixteenth century, so my father was told when he first bought it. My husband planned to delve more into the history of it but he didn't have time...I mean, he never got around to it.'

There was an awkward pause which Jackie filled by pressing down the handle of the passenger door and leaping out. She was sure that someone at the surgery would have mentioned David's death to Tom Prestwick this morning so it shouldn't have come as a surprise that she was a widow.

It was one of the first pieces of information that her friends and colleagues passed on to newcomers, usually filling in the details about how David had died. Sometimes she felt it was pure sensationalism but she'd learned to live with it. When your husband had been labelled a hero you had to put up with the natural curiosity of people who were unfamiliar with the facts.

She slotted her key in the door. 'Do come in, Dr Prestwick.'

'Do you think you could call me Tom, as we're going to be colleagues?'

She turned round and smiled. 'I'd like that.' And the amazing thing was that she really meant it! In spite of his overpowering confidence—or perhaps because of it—she found herself wanting to get to know this man. Not that she would allow it to lead anywhere...

'Why don't you call me Jackie?' She kept her voice deliberately light as she went into the oak beamed kitchen.

'Mind your head on the— Oh, dear, too late!'

'Ouch!' Tom's handsome features were screwed up into an agonised grimace as he rubbed the top of his head where it had made contact with the low oak beam above the doorway.

'Here, bend down and let me have a look.'

He gave her a wry grin as he stooped and presented the top of his head.

'Good thing you've got thick hair.'

She rubbed her hand gently over the rough-textured strands, her fingers probing lightly to see if the skin had been broken. To her utter dismay, she felt a curious sensation as her fingers made contact with Tom's skin. She was actually enjoying this physical contact with a perfect stranger!

She drew in her breath. 'No harm done,' she said briskly. 'Why don't you wait in the dining room while I check on the bathroom shower unit to see if the plumber's been? But do mind your head as you go through the doorway. They were very small people in the sixteenth century.'

She ran up the stairs. Inside the bathroom was a note and a bill from the plumber. Excellent! She could go out to lunch without delay. She glanced in the mirror and dragged out hairpins from her chignon. What a mess it looked. She was surprised that a sophisticated man like Tom Prestwick would dare to be seen out with her.

Quickly she brushed out her long hair. It trailed over her shoulders. Perhaps she should get the ends cut some time soon. She reached for the chignon shaper so that she could pull her hair through the middle and wind it round the sides.

The phone was ringing. The nearest one was on the landing. Hair flapping around her shoulders, she answered it.

'Hello... Yes, Rosemary... Yes, of course I realise you can't leave little Susan if she's got a temperature... No, that's OK, I'll cope with this afternoon's clinic and...'

Looking down the stairs, she saw that Tom Prestwick had wandered out of the dining room and was looking up at her. She finished speaking and frowned as she put the phone down.

'Problems?' Tom asked.

She went slowly down towards him and sat on one of the steps halfway down.

'Rosemary has got her little girl at home ill. It doesn't sound serious but she can't leave her this afternoon so I'll have to take the mother and baby clinic on my own.'

He stood at the bottom of the stairs, his long, athletic legs firmly apart and his hands on his hips as he gave her a confident smile.

'I'd like to work in the clinic with you this afternoon.'

She went down the last few stairs and stood looking up at him. My God, he was tall!

'I'm not sure how the women would take it. It's always been a completely feminine afternoon. The mothers never wanted Dr Vickers to be anywhere around.'

He shrugged his broad shoulders. 'I'm not Dr Vickers and, don't forget, I used to specialise in obstetrics and gynaecology. As I told you at the interview, I was considering becoming a consultant...before I changed my mind.'

For a few seconds his expressive brown eyes held a troubled expression.

'Yes, I remember,' she said quietly. 'That must have been some big decision to throw all that up and go into general practice.'

He stroked his chin thoughtfully.

'That's what life's all about, isn't it? Decisions. I've always found that there are two kinds you have to deal with. Big ones and little ones. You shouldn't need to agonise over the little ones, whereas you have to weigh up all the pros and cons with big decisions...and they're very hard to make.'

He paused and looked down at her, a vulnerable expression in his eyes. 'I hope I'm not boring you.'

She shook her head. She found she enjoyed listening to the sound of his voice. It was husky now, as if he was reaching deep down into his very soul, searching for the truth.

'Sometimes you just have to convince yourself that a big decision is really not so big after all. Then you've got to go for it. Take a step in the dark.'

She would have liked to ask him why he'd had to make this big decision, but she felt he'd already revealed more to her than he'd meant to. They'd only just met and it was unusual for two people to start baring their souls so early on in a relationship.

Heavens! Was she planning a relationship? No, of course she wasn't. But it would be nice to have a good atmosphere when they were working together.

'It would definitely be a help to have you with me for the mother and baby clinic,' she said quickly. 'I'll just go and finish my hair.'

'It's a pity you have to twine it all up again,' he said quietly.

She stopped on the bottom step, alarmed that he'd actually reached out to touch her hair.

'You look so much younger with it casually round your shoulders. So much more...approachable.'

She turned and saw an expression of something which might be admiration in his eyes. Standing on the bottom step meant that her eyes were level with his. She gave a nervous laugh.

'I could hardly wear it like this in the surgery. It would be so unhygienic.'

He put both hands on her shoulders and looked directly into her eyes.

'Of course it would, Doctor. Unhygienic...but very attractive.'

As he spoke she could feel his warm breath fanning her face. There was a delicious smell of expensive cologne wafting in the air. She hadn't stood this close to a man in this sort of electrically charged situation for years.

She knew she ought to move away but she felt strangely excited.

'Perhaps you'd better go and imprison your hair again,' he said. 'It's far too distracting.'

Why did she feel such a sense of disappointment as she ran back up the stairs? What had she been waiting for? She didn't dare to admit it, even to herself!

CHAPTER TWO

THE Smugglers Inn was packed with lunchtime drinkers, propping up the bar and crowding around the tables as Tom pushed open the heavy, ancient door. He turned to look at Jackie and pulled a wry face.

'It's a bit of a crush in there. Shall we find somewhere quieter?'

She shook her head. 'No, this is fine.'

She knew she would enjoy being part of the anonymity of the crowd. At the moment she needed lots of background noise to cover the unnerving feelings which had crept over her as Tom had driven down to Estersea. She wasn't used to going out to lunch with an unfamiliar man. And she wanted to see if she could go into this pub again after all those years. It was a challenge she had to face.

She put a hand on her hair. The chignon was still in place, which was amazing considering the alacrity with which she'd accomplished the task of retwining her hair in her haste to be out of the house. The compromising nature of the situation had hit her with full force as she'd run back up the stairs to the bathroom.

Tom pursed his lips. 'Well, on your head be it. There's a table over by the window. Put your hands against my back and I'll find a way through this scrum. I used to be a rugby forward so we should make it.'

Momentarily, Jackie hesitated, before putting her hands on the fine, expensive cloth of Tom's jacket. She couldn't help but be aware of the strong muscles hidden beneath as she followed him, finding it easy to imagine him on the rugby field. He certainly had the required physique. She allowed herself to be drawn through the chattering crowd towards a recently vacated table. Tom carried the empty beer glasses and overflowing ashtray to the bar, returning with two glasses of white wine.

He eased himself down beside her on the wooden bench. 'I've ordered the dish of the day—fish pie. Is that OK for you?'

'Fine!'

She had a sip of wine as she took a tentative glance out of the window. Down by the harbour the seagulls were weaving and diving over the fishing boats. Further along the quay she could see the place where her parents used to moor their boat. A lump rose in her throat and she deliberately turned her back on the scene. She'd trained herself not to grieve any more.

'The fish should be fresh if it was bought locally,' Tom was saying.

'Yes, it's a speciality in this area.'

They were polite strangers again and Jackie felt a certain amount of relief. The close contact as they'd pushed through the crowd had disturbed her more than she cared to admit.

A barman was waving at Tom, indicating that their food was ready. Jackie watched as he made his way over to the bar, a tall, athletic figure in a charcoal grey suit, easing his way through. He had a certain distinguished air about him. Yes, he would have made a good consultant. Whatever had made him change his plans?

'Wow, the plates are hot! Be careful.'

Tom was laughing as he plonked the plates on the table, before rubbing his hands together.

'Mmm, delicious!' Jackie savoured the flavour of fresh cod in a white sauce, topped with creamed potatoes and garnished with prawns and a flourish of parsley.

'Haven't been in this pub for ages. I used to come in as a child with my parents and sit in the family room through that door. And then later, when Dad retired from the practice and they bought the boat—Dad's pride and joy—I used to bring the twins down for a lemonade and meet them coming back from...'

She put down her fork as she struggled to finish the sentence. Tom was watching her, his brown, expressive eyes full of concern.

She took a deep breath and her voice came out stronger. 'You see, four years ago my parents didn't come back from one of their trips. There was a sudden storm, and apparently their boat capsized. I was waiting here with Debbie and Fiona when the coastguard came to bring me the news that the lifeboat was bringing in their bodies.'

The concern in Tom's eyes deepened and he put out a hand to cover hers. She knew it was simply the automatic gesture of a sympathetic doctor and she found it very comforting. Too comforting, in fact, because she hated people to pity her.

'I'm so sorry, Jackie. I wouldn't have suggested this place if I'd known. You should have told me.'

'I wanted to come in. It's good for me to be here.' She forced herself to smile as their eyes met across the table.

'Do I get the impression you like jumping over hurdles?' he said slowly as he removed his hand, his expressive brown eyes scanning her face in an unnerving manner.

She looked down at her plate and picked up her fork again. 'Especially when the hurdles taste as good as this,' she said quickly, trying to lighten the mood again.

He was smiling again. 'You're a survivor, aren't you, Jackie?'

'Aren't we all?' she said, a little too glibly. She'd got used to covering up her feelings, blanking out her emotions.

She finished every last scrap of the delicious concoction and put down her fork. Glancing idly across the room, she could see through the open door of the family room to the children's bar. Two familiar figures were now sitting on high stools, sipping Coca-Cola through long straws.

'Oh, no!' She clapped a hand to her face.

'What's the matter?'

'My daughters are in the children's room.'

His face lit up with interest and curiosity as he followed the direction of her eyes. 'Well, let's go and see them.'

'No! I mean, they wouldn't understand why I was here with...'

He smiled. 'Too late—they've seen us.'

He was already standing up. 'Come on, Jackie. I'd love to meet them.'

She was very much aware that he was right behind her as she led the way through into the junior bar. The girls' faces were a picture of surprise as she walked in with the hand-some stranger.

'Hello! How was the cookery lesson?' she said brightly, forcing a smile.

Dark-haired Deborah put her Coca-Cola down on the bar and looked up at Jackie, surreptitiously sneaking a glance at the unknown man standing behind her.

'Not too bad. We can have my cake for tea. But Fiona's cake—'

'My cake sank in the middle,' fair-haired Fiona inter-rupted, pulling a wry face. 'But don't worry, Mum, I bor-rowed some jam and sort of filled it in. It's not a total disaster but—'

'Can't wait to taste it!' Jackie said quickly. 'This is Dr Prestwick, who's just joined the practice. We're having a working lunch.'

'How do you do, sir?'

The girls' response came out in unison. Jackie wasn't fooled by their tone of ultra-politeness. It had been five years since David had died and they still guarded his memory jeal-ously. It must have come as a shock for them to see her out with Tom, considering she hadn't even thought about going out with a man since she'd been widowed. Well, she was a bit surprised herself.

Fiona climbed down from her stool, smoothing her hands over her navy blue school skirt.

'Heavens, is that the time? If we don't get a move on we'll be late for our first lesson.'

'Why don't I run you back to school?' Tom said, pulling his car keys from his pocket. 'Jackie and I have finished our lunch and we need to get back to work.'

Jackie saw the look that passed between her daughters when Tom said, 'Jackie and I'. She realised that they'd all got so used to their totally female family life that they simply weren't used to having a man amongst them.

'What a good idea!' she said quickly, walking with her daughters towards the outer door. 'Then you'll be sure to be on time.'

Back at the car, Tom opened the rear passenger door. 'Debbie and Fiona in the back, I think.'

'I'll explain the way to our school, Dr Prestwick,' Debbie said as Tom moved out of the car park.

'That's OK. Your mother pointed it out to me when we drove down.'

Jackie glanced sideways, her eyes pleading with him not to mention the fact that she'd ducked her head and crouched down in her seat in case they'd been out in the playground. He was grinning mischievously, but he remained silent. For an instant he took his eyes off the road and she smiled at him, before turning away.

There was a certain rapport growing between them and she wasn't sure how she should handle it. She'd only known this man for a few hours and already he was having a strange effect on her. On the one hand she was trying to hold him at arm's length and on the other she was actually enjoying his company.

Perhaps Helen had been right when she'd advised her to go out more. She shouldn't read too much into her change of mood. It was obviously more exciting to go out for a pub lunch than sit at home with a cheese sandwich!

Tom pulled up outside the school and the girls got out. As they went through the gates Debbie turned round and waved. Jackie waved back. Fiona hurried on ahead.

Jackie sat back and looked out of the window as they drove. They were passing the new medical centre. The builders were still working on it, but it looked as if it would soon be finished.

'Impressive building!' Tom said, slowing the car down so that he could get a better look at it. 'I read about it in *The Times*, the other day. A purpose-built medical centre for Estersea and the surrounding areas, it said. How will that affect the Benton practice?'

'I've had a letter to say that I'll be able to make use of the new medical facilities when I need to—send patients for X-rays, blood tests and so on. It will save them from having to travel to Colchester. And there's going to be a prenatal clinic with all the latest medical technology.'

'Well, I'll certainly want to make use of it,' Tom said enthusiastically, his eyes staring straight ahead at the road. 'It's good to have all the latest technology near at hand. I mean, with respect, from what I've seen so far, the Benton practice is a bit old-fashioned, isn't it?'

She bridled at his unsolicited criticism of her beloved practice.

'Tom, our family practice is concerned with much more than the latest technology. There's been a tradition in our family to give warm, hands-on care to our patients. I'll use the facilities as a back-up but not as a substitute for good old-fashioned doctoring.'

'I think the two can go hand in hand,' he said firmly. 'It's a question of getting the right balance.'

She saw his hands tighten on the wheel. A muscle was quivering in his jaw and she sensed the underlying tension that threatened to explode. She wondered if he resented the fact that she was the senior partner in the practice.

'I expect you err on the side of technology, don't you?' she said quietly.

He was steering the car round a sharp bend and for a few seconds he didn't speak. When he did, his words came out in a deliberately measured tone.

'It would depend on the medical case. Look, let's drop it, shall we? You've made it obvious where you stand. Let's just agree to differ.'

It took all her powers of self-control not to make a retort; but, having spent her lunchtime trying to create a good working relationship with Tom, she didn't want to blow it by provoking a confrontation. It was perfectly obvious that he wasn't going to make any concession to the fact that she was senior partner.

They were approaching the surgery when Tom broke the silence.

'I enjoyed meeting your daughters, but I thought they seemed a bit wary of me at first.'

'That's understandable. They're not used to having men around, and you're the first they've seen with me in public in five years. It's as simple as that.'

He raised an eyebrow. 'I wouldn't call that simple. Five years is a long time to remain cloistered at home. Haven't you ever wanted to go out with a man?'

'No, I haven't,' she said quickly. 'I'm perfectly happy and fulfilled with my life as it is. I've got the girls, I've got a rewarding job, I—'

'Fine! If you're happy, that's the main thing.'

As he slowed down, approaching the surgery car park, he took his eyes from the wheel to glance at her with an enigmatic expression on his face.

'If you'd like to move your car back into its number one space...'

'I'll leave it there for the afternoon,' she said hastily. 'You can park in my space.'

He swung the car into space number one and switched off the engine. She pushed open the door and hurried across to the surgery.

Jackie was relieved to find that Helen had everything under control. Four mothers had arrived early with their babies and Helen was dispensing the tea and biscuits, which was one of the highlights of this particular clinic.

On some occasions Jackie felt it was more of a social event than a medical clinic. The mothers always turned out in full force, and she was sure that a good gossip between women in the same situation was very therapeutic. Some of the mothers would stay all afternoon until Helen had to gently nudge them out to make room for the others who were still waiting to be seen.

'Hello, ladies,' Jackie said, walking across the tiled floor to retrieve one of the foam toy building bricks.

She tossed the brick back into the playpen for the waiting toddler, who was howling loudly as he grasped the side of the playpen and jigged up and down impatiently. The little boy pounced on the precious brick and the howls turned to laughter.

'I'd like to introduce Dr Prestwick, who's going to see some of you this afternoon.'

She had an anxious moment as she watched the four mothers make a quick appraisal of the new doctor. Their faces registered approval—in fact, more than approval! She could see that they were positively smitten by this handsome new man! Even Amelia Jones, who was breast-feeding her baby in the corner of the room, didn't bat an eyelid at this intrusion into their usually female domain.

Jackie glanced at Tom and saw that he appeared to be

perfectly at home. He was, after all, she reminded herself, used to obstetrics and gynaecology so it was all routine to him.

'OK, Dr Prestwick and I will disappear into our rooms now and Helen will let you know when it's your turn to come and see us. We'll try not to keep you waiting too long because I know you all want to get home as soon as you can.'

She glanced at Helen who was smiling at this last remark.

'You must be joking!' Helen said quietly, as Jackie started up the stairs to her room.

Jackie smiled. 'Well, there's no harm in dropping a hint.'

But as she went into her room she was thinking how nice it was to have such a relaxed attitude in her clinic. It was good for the mothers to get out and meet other mothers. A happy mother would be a healthy mother, and a healthy mother would be a good mother to her children.

The door opened. 'I couldn't knock, Doctor. Not with Lucy in my arms.'

'No, of course you couldn't, Amelia.' Jackie stood up and crossed the room to meet her patient. 'Let me hold Lucy for you. Oh, isn't she adorable? Who's a beautiful little girl, then?'

'Look, she's smiling at you, Doctor. That's not wind, you know.'

'She's going to break a few hearts when she grows up,' Jackie said, smiling at the tiny child in her arms. 'I'll put her down in the cot here. You've just fed her, haven't you? Oh, that was a nice big burp, Lucy.'

'It's all over your jacket, Doctor.'

'Oh, not to worry.' Jackie reached for a tissue with the hand that wasn't holding the baby and dabbed at the sticky mess on her shoulder.

Another jacket for the dry-cleaners! Still, it was all part of the job. She should have taken the jacket off sooner. She

settled the baby in the cot, removed her jacket and put on a
clean white coat, before glancing at Amelia's notes.

'You've come for your six-week check-up, haven't you,
Amelia? How've you been since I last saw you?'

'Fine. Tired, of course, but that's babies for you, isn't it?
Oh, for a good night's sleep! Look at the little tinker. Fast
asleep now, but wait until tonight—it'll be a different story!
I walked the bedroom floor with her from midnight until four
o'clock and Malcolm moved into the spare room.'

'Do you think Lucy was hungry?' Jackie asked.

'Well, I had nothing left to give her.'

'That could be the problem. Perhaps you need to sup-
plement her feeds with a bottle occasionally.'

Amelia smiled. 'I wouldn't mind that because I could hand
her over to Malcolm. Then I could be the one to complain
if she wasn't sleeping!'

'After I've examined you I'll weigh Lucy. And I'd also
like to analyse a specimen of your milk. If you could express
a sample into this bottle, up to the line there, I'd be able to
tell you if there's any problem.'

After examining Amelia, Jackie was able to reassure her
that she was in excellent shape internally.

'So normal services can be resumed as soon as possible,
can they, Doctor?' Amelia asked, with a little giggle.

Jackie smiled. 'They certainly can. I'm surprised you
waited this long. I know that's what we doctors usually ad-
vise, but that's only in our professional capacity. Most patients seem to take the matter into their own hands.'

'Malcolm's been champing at the bit but I wanted to be
sure. And I've been so tired I haven't felt like it.'

'I can see that what you need is a good night's sleep. I'll
weigh young Lucy now.'

The scales showed that Lucy wasn't putting on enough
weight so Jackie advised supplementary feeds with a bottle.

'Drop the milk specimen into the surgery as soon as you

can. In fact, if you go and have another cup of tea you could probably leave it here at the end of the afternoon—that's if you've got time, Amelia.'

'Oh, I've got plenty of time. It's nice to get out of the house for a change.'

The afternoon had seemed to fly. It appeared as if one minute she was seeing her first patient and the next she was closing the door on the last. In between, she'd fitted a couple of contraceptive coils, examined and referred three patients to the fertility clinic, weighed, examined and admired several babies, as well as handing out repeat prescriptions and new medication for a variety of ailments after long and lengthy discussions—all interspersed with chat and laughter.

'Busy?' Tom poked his head round the door.

She glanced away from her computer screen. 'Just putting the final notes on file. How did you get on this afternoon?'

'Fine! I enjoyed it. You know, you've got a nice set-up here, Jackie. Very relaxed, which is what you need with gynae and obstetric patients.'

'So you didn't find it a problem that we're short on the high-tech equipment?' she asked.

He came towards her desk and leaned against the back of one of the patients' chairs, his expression suddenly very serious.

'Let's say that it wouldn't do any harm to consider making a few improvements in our equipment. I know I'm the new boy here, but I'd like to make a few changes.'

'And I'm perfectly happy with the way the surgery runs now,' Jackie said, her firm tone belying the fact that Tom was making her feel strangely nervous. 'You knew we were an old established family practice when you applied to come here, Tom, and—'

He interrupted her, running a hand through his dark brown hair in a gesture of frustration.

'Jackie, there's no need to be so touchy. You asked my opinion, remember?'

She flinched at the angry expression on his face. 'The three of us can have a discussion about changes when Meg gets back,' she said evenly.

He pursed his lips. 'And shelve the idea?'

She drew in her breath. How had he managed to read her mind? She was perfectly happy with the way things had always been.

'Not necessarily,' she said quietly.

He stood and looked down at her, as if deciding whether it was worth pursuing the argument. Suddenly he shrugged and turned away.

'Well, if you don't need me any more today I'll go off home.'

'Where's home?' She realised that she was trying to keep him here longer. She didn't want them to part on a sour note.

He turned back, his eyes once more friendly as he looked at her.

'I've taken a little house in Estersea, overlooking the water—not very far from the pub where we had lunch, actually. It doesn't feel much like home yet, but it will seem less impersonal when I've hung a few of my pictures around the place and made some shelves for my books.'

He paused and leaned forward across her desk, the expression in his eyes becoming decidedly warmer.

'If you'd like to see the place I'll invite you to supper one evening.'

'That would be nice.'

What was she saying? Even in a crowded pub she'd found him strangely disturbing. 'But on second thoughts...'

He gave her a wry grin. 'You should never have second thoughts. The first thoughts are the ones you really believe in. See you tomorrow, Jackie.'

She listened as the sound of his footsteps echoed away

down the stairs. She reached forward, switched off the computer and leaned back in her chair, wondering how she was going to cope with having Tom around her. He'd definitely been the best candidate for the job on paper but the reality was already more disturbing than she'd imagined.

For a couple of weeks, whenever she thought about it, she wondered what she should say if Tom did ask her to his place for supper.

The idea intrigued her. There were so many aspects of his life that puzzled her and it would be good to talk things over and find out more about him, but it had been so long since she'd been alone with a man that she didn't know if she could handle it.

Sitting at her desk and waiting for the first patient to arrive, she leaned forward and pulled off the leaf from her daily calendar. The first of June. The last few days had been very hot and humid. Even with the windows wide open, her consulting room felt stuffy. Maybe she should think about air-conditioning. Many of the larger group practices were having it installed for the summer.

She knew what her father would have said about the idea—a shameful waste of money that could be much better spent!

Someone knocked on her door.

'Come in!'

'I knocked in case you had a patient with you.'

Tom came over to the desk and leaned across towards her. He was wearing one of his smooth, consultant-type suits. Very expensive! Where on earth did he get the money from? He obviously didn't have any family commitments to drain away his salary.

As he smiled down at her she noticed how strong and white his teeth were. In the two weeks he'd been out here in the country his skin had acquired a light suntan, which suited him. She knew he was keen on spending time outdoors during his off-duty.

'How are you fixed for tonight? I've got the house fairly shipshape and I'd like you to come for supper.'

'Not tonight,' she heard herself say.

She knew she should be adding, 'or any other night,' but some little demon was holding her back.

His brow creased. 'Tomorrow, then?'

She shook her head, trying to convince herself she'd made the right decision. Knock the idea on the head before it became an issue.

'Tom, in the evenings I always like to make sure the girls get started with their homework. Then we cook supper together and—'

'Sounds deadly boring to me. What you mean is you don't want to make the effort to go out.'

He pulled a wry face as he looked down at her, scrutinising her in an unnerving way.

She shifted her position on her chair. 'It's not the effort involved, it's...'

She paused as she desperately searched her mind for something that would convince Tom she had a cast-iron reason for not going down to look at his house.

His full, expressive mouth twitched at the corners, before breaking out into a knowing smile. He raised one eyebrow as he continued to look down at her.

'You've dried up, haven't you? Run out of excuses. Why don't you take a couple of minutes to think it over?'

He moved from the desk and went over to the window, looking out at the trees in the practice garden and beyond to the fields. After a few seconds he broke the silence, making no attempt to disguise his impatience.

'Jackie, I'm not asking you for anything, except the pleasure of your company for a couple of hours. Anyone would think I was setting up a seduction scenario!' he added in a whimsical tone.

She laughed. 'Well, maybe it would do me good to get out for a change, and I'd certainly like to see your house, so...'

He swung round, his face wreathed in smiles. 'That's better.'

He strode across the room and put his hands on her shoulders.

She held her breath at the proximity of him. The sensible half of her wished he wouldn't do that! She could feel a certain thawing of emotions she didn't want to admit still existed. But the other, wayward half relished his nearness and the new, exciting sensations it evoked.

'Can you make it by eight?'

The intercom buzzed. 'Your first patient is here, Dr Brent, and Dr Prestwick's patient is already in his room. Will you be long in conference?'

Jackie smiled as she heard Helen's exaggerated professional tone.

Tom grinned. 'Helen likes to keep her finger on the pulse, doesn't she? I'd better go.'

Jackie's first patient was a dear little blond-haired five-year-old boy in blue denim dungarees and a bright red shirt.

'He can't stop sneezing, Dr Brent,' the tired-looking mother said. 'Now, don't wander off, Mark. Doctor wants to have a look at you.'

'That's OK, Mrs Trimble. Let him have a play while we chat about this.'

Young Mark had made a beeline for Jackie's toy corner and was already running a smart-looking car over the tiles.

'Brrm-brrm...'

'You say Mark can't stop sneezing. He seems OK at the moment.'

Mrs Trimble settled her ample figure into a more comfortable position on the wooden chair. 'That's because he's finished sneezing for the morning. First thing in the morning he's terrible! I just can't get him ready for school, and some days he sneezes himself into a nosebleed so I have to keep him at home.'

'When did he start school?'

'Easter, Doctor.'

'And is he happy there?'

Mrs Trimble looked puzzled. She thought for a few moments. 'Well, he didn't like it at first but he's fairly resigned to it now. What's that got to do with his nose?'

'I'm just checking to see if there's an underlying reason why he might get these sneezing attacks. We need to consider every possible cause. Let me have a look at Mark now.'

Mark, totally oblivious to everything except the cars and the miniature petrol station, reluctantly left his game and allowed Jackie to do a thorough examination of his ears, nose, throat and chest.

Jackie put down her stethoscope when she'd finished. 'What a good boy you are, Mark! Do you want to carry on playing now?'

Didn't he just! Jackie explained to his mother that there was nothing physically wrong with his upper respiratory system but she wanted to do a series of tests to check out if he was allergic to something.

'If you'd like to go and see Sister in the treatment room downstairs she'll check Mark out for allergies. He may be allergic to any number of things—pollen, grass, dust...'

'There's no dust in my house, Doctor! I keep the cleanest house in Benton.'

'I'm sure you do, Mrs Trimble,' Jackie said hastily. 'But we can't totally rid ourselves of the dust in our environment, and some people can't cope with it. Mark may be one of them. The tests that Sister's going to do will show up any substances he's allergic to. When we have a clearer picture, we could start to desensitise him against these things, if necessary.'

Mrs Trimble smiled. 'Well, I feel a lot happier than when I came in, Doctor. Children can be such a worry, can't they? How are your little girls these days?'

'Not so little, Mrs Trimble! Debbie's taller than me and Fiona's only a little bit shorter.'

'I always thought it was strange them being so different when they're twins. Non-identical, it's called, isn't it? How old are they now?'

'Sixteen.'

'Goodness me, doesn't time fly?'

'It does indeed, Mrs Trimble.'

Time continued to fly throughout the day, bringing Jackie inexorably nearer to her date with Tom. Whenever she had a minute to herself between patients she found she was anxiously mentally reviewing her wardrobe—or rather the lack of it!

What on earth should she wear? She had serviceable workday suits, woollen dresses, last year's cotton frock—yes, just the one that she'd bought at the Benton fair from a visiting trader she'd felt sorry for.

It had been a hot day, she remembered, as she leaned back in her chair and allowed her thoughts to wander. She'd been doing her dutiful rounds of the stalls in her capacity of village doctor. Her father and grandfather had always patronised the annual summer fair and so she'd had to step into their shoes. She'd spent something on every stall—even won a goldfish.

She'd been carrying the poor little captive fish in his small jamjar, holding tightly to the string handle, when she'd spotted a young couple with a whole row of ethnic-type dresses on an iron rail.

'Hand-made in Bali,' the young man had told her, hoisting

his delightfully decked-out toddler onto his knee. 'Going cheap, this lot, because it's the end of the day.'

The little girl on his lap had gravely wiped her lollipop across the front of her frilly dress and held it out towards Jackie.

The man had laughed. 'I think Emmy wants you to have a lick, missis.'

She'd smiled at the little girl and admired the large floppy hat that threatened to envelop her completely.

'I won't have a lick, thank you, but I'll buy one of Daddy's dresses. Which one shall I have?'

The little girl had leapt down off her dad's knee, toddled over to the rack of dresses and stuck the lollipop against a green and yellow flowered cotton dress.

'You can have vat one.'

And so it was that Jackie had parted with twenty-five pounds and had reminded herself, as the trader had put the dress in a plastic Tesco bag, that he'd needed the money more than she had.

Amazingly, she'd enjoyed wearing this rather way-out creation—but only at home, in the garden on warm summer evenings. It had made her feel sort of abandoned, definitely different—and younger.

But was it suitable for tonight and, more importantly, dare she wear it?

It was seven-thirty and she still hadn't come to a decision about what to wear. She'd told Debbie and Fiona she was going to be out for a couple of hours and had written Tom's phone number on the noticeboard in the kitchen. If they'd been surprised they hadn't said anything—yet!

The girls were downstairs now at the kitchen table, doing their homework.

On impulse, she reached for the green and yellow flowered

dress from the back of the wardrobe. Pulling it over her head, she did a quick twirl in front of the mirror.

Yes, maybe this was, after all, the dress for tonight. It did something for her. It was certainly hot enough to warrant wearing a sleeveless dress. She fastened all the buttons down the front. Perhaps she would have to leave the bottom two at the hem of the skirt undone when she was driving...but do them up before she got out of the car so that—

'You can't wear that!' Fiona, standing in the doorway, was looking askance at her mother.

Jackie flinched, but stuck out her jaw defiantly. 'Why not?'

Fiona gave a toss of her long blonde hair. 'Because...because it makes you look like...well, it's too young for you.'

'Fiona, I'm thirty-four.'

'Exactly!'

For a brief instant Jackie was tempted to pick up the phone and cancel the whole thing. It was all such a hassle! But a small voice inside her head told her she ought to make the effort.

Reaching into her wardrobe, she pulled out her old dirndl skirt and selected a clean white blouse.

'How about this?' she asked her daughter.

Fiona smiled and nodded. 'You always look nice in that, Mum.'

Jackie tossed away the little made-in-Bali number. Not for her the exotic trappings of the Far East!

'Glad you could make it,' Tom said, opening the door and letting out a delicious smell of cooking.

He looked so different in well-cut jeans and an open-necked shirt. Casual clothes suited him even more than his smart, daytime suits.

'Come through into the kitchen.'

She followed him along a narrow hallway, open doors on

each side giving glimpses of newly painted sitting and dining rooms, to a large, bright, airy kitchen. The windows were wide open, making the most of the glorious view over the estuary. She could see seagulls, ducking and diving over the water.

'What a wonderful situation!' She leaned out through the window.

A couple of swans were gliding sedately past, followed by five brown cygnets, their feathers fluffed out in the warm summer breeze.

He took a bottle of white wine from the fridge and placed it on the kitchen table, which was directly in front of the window.

'Come and sit down, Jackie. You look as if you need a drink.'

Was that Tom-speak for how frumpy she looked? She settled herself at the table and took the glass he held out to her.

'Thanks. I mustn't drink more than one glass because of the driving.'

'Of course. I've got some mineral water, chilling in the fridge.'

'You're very organised for a...for a bachelor.'

He gave her a long slow smile. 'What makes you think I'm a bachelor?'

'Well, as far as I can see, there's no Mrs Prestwick in tow.'

He pulled a wry face. 'There was, but we decided to part.'

'Oh, I'm sorry.'

'I'm not! It wasn't working out.'

He reached across the table. 'Let me top up your glass... Oh, no, you're driving, aren't you?'

He went over to the fridge and took out a bottle of mineral water. His back was towards her but she could tell he was disturbed about something, which was unusual for him. In the two weeks she'd known him he'd always been totally in control.

'These things happen.' She was trying to sound sympathetic about his unsuccessful marriage.

He came back to the table, once more his usual confident self. She wondered if his marriage split had been the reason for him leaving London.

'I enjoy being by myself,' he said. 'It gives me the time to do the things I want to do.'

'Such as?'

'I love painting.'

He leaned back in the wooden kitchen chair. 'If I hadn't desperately wanted to be a doctor, I'd have liked to have been an artist. My father was exactly the same. He spent all his off-duty time painting, and Mum insisted on hanging his paintings all over the surgery.'

'I didn't know your father was a doctor.'

He smiled. 'There's a lot you don't know about me. Dad was a GP in Yorkshire until he died a few years ago. Mum still lives in the house where we had the practice but it's long since been superseded by a large group surgery in a modern, purpose-built building in the centre of the village.'

'Have you got any of your paintings here? I'd love to see them.'

He gave her a rakish grin. 'Is this the reverse of, "Come up and see my etchings"?'

To her horror she could feel herself blushing. 'I'm just curious, that's all.'

Oh, what a tame reply that sounded, even to her own ears! She was so out of practice in dealing with quick-witted men. She hoped he hadn't really thought she—

'I keep my paintings in what the estate agent called the wash-house. It's actually the best room for light—and inspiration, for that matter—because it looks out over the water. Come and have a look.'

She forgot her embarrassment as she looked at Tom's paintings in the whitewashed room adjacent to the kitchen. Even with her limited knowledge of the subject, she could see he had talent. She particularly admired the half-finished painting on an easel in front of the window, which portrayed the swans and their cygnets. She looked out across the water.

'They're still there. Do you want to do some more work on the painting tonight, Tom?'

He smiled. 'Far more important things to think about to-night.'

He put his hand on her shoulder and guided her back into the kitchen. 'More important things, like rescuing the chicken casserole before it gets too charred.'

He whipped open the oven door. 'I hope you like well-browned chicken.'

She laughed. 'It smells delicious.'

The casserole, although overcooked, tasted wonderful.

'It's so relaxing to come out and not have to organise the cooking. The girls are very good at helping but I always feel I've got to stay in charge in case anything goes wrong.'

'Did you have to cook before you came out this evening?'

'No, it's Fiona's turn tonight. She's going to do pasta and tuna-fish. Nothing much can go wrong with that.'

'Followed by her disastrous cake?' Tom said, an amused smile hovering on his lips.

Jackie laughed. 'Not if Debbie can help it!'

'You've got a nice family, Jackie. And you seem to have your family life well organised. It's good to let teenagers help in running the home. If kids are spoiled and aren't ex-pected to make a contribution to the family life they can get away with murder.'

She felt the old familiar pain shoot through her. Murder...those awful headlines. She put a hand up to her temple to soothe away the throbbing.

'Jackie, what is it? Was it something I said? I didn't mean to…'

'No, of course you didn't.'

He was crouching beside her, taking hold of her hands and pulling her towards him. She didn't resist. It was wonderful to feel the strength of him. She leaned against him and, unwittingly, her face made contact with the gap in his cotton shirt where the buttons were gaping awry. His skin felt warm and soothing and the faint male scent excited her. She closed her eyes.

Seconds later she opened them again. What on earth was she doing in this compromising position?

'I'm OK now.' She pulled herself away.

'Then why the tears?' he asked gently.

He stood up and walked back to his seat. 'Would you like to talk about it?'

She hesitated. 'It was when you said the word 'murder'. It always affects me since David was killed. All those headlines in the newspapers. It was so awful! I suppose someone must have told you all about it by now. It's usually the first topic of conversation when somebody new comes to join the practice.'

He looked puzzled. 'As a matter of fact, they haven't. Well, Helen simply said your husband died five years ago, but that was all. And, of course, I didn't ask any questions.'

'No. Of course you wouldn't. But lots of people do. Helen must have curbed her love of sensationally dramatising the situation. I have, on occasions, told her that I wish everyone would stop talking about it.'

She looked across at Tom. His eyes were full of sympathy but he remained silent.

She took a deep breath. 'David was in the surgery one evening. Dr Meg Gresham was also there in her own consulting room. They'd shared the evening surgery.'

'Dr Gresham is the doctor who's on holiday at the moment, isn't she?'

'Yes, she always goes to the Greek islands in the spring for a month. She'll be back in the surgery tomorrow.'

She paused. 'I don't know for sure what exactly happened that night. Meg always maintains that David saved her life. She'd been about to go home when the door of her consulting room burst open and a youth came in and threatened her with a knife. He demanded drugs. She told him she didn't have any in her room. He frogmarched her along the corridor towards the dispensary and...'

Suddenly she couldn't go on.

Tom leaned across the table and took hold of her hands. 'And your husband heard the noise, I suppose, and came to the rescue.'

His voice was very understanding. She looked up and nodded, her eyes brimming with tears.

'David tackled the youth, apparently, and got knifed in the back when the youth panicked and ran off. Meg phoned for the ambulance, then called me. I went to the hospital and arrived...just before David died.'

Tom stood up and slowly moved around the table. Gently he pulled her to her feet and folded her in his arms.

'If there's ever anything I can do to ease the pain... I'm glad you told me because now I'm beginning to understand what you've been through.'

He bent his head. She saw his lips hovering above her. She hoped he would kiss her. It would be such a comfort. As his lips touched her cheek, oh, so gently, she felt an overwhelming sense of peace. But was it peace she was searching for, or did she want to extend the feeling of excitement that being near Tom evoked?

A feeling of guilt swept over her. How could she think of such a thing only seconds after she'd been talking about David? She pulled herself away.

'David was hailed as a hero,' she said quickly, her voice shaky and breathless. 'He won a posthumous award for bravery.'

He nodded. 'I seem to remember reading about it in the press, but I'd forgotten about it and I hadn't connected it with the Benton surgery.'

'The girls are so proud of their hero father,' she said, trying to calm her churning emotions.

'Quite something to live up to,' he said evenly.

'They certainly think so.'

'And so do you, Jackie,' he said quietly.

'Yes.'

She knew she'd idolised her husband's memory for the last five years, but not with the same blind faith of her daughters. For some unknown reason she had a tiny reservation about it.

It had something to do with the time she'd spent with David in hospital just before he'd died. Something had disturbed her but she'd been in such a state of shock that she could never remember what it was.

'Coffee?'

Tom's voice broke through her reverie. She looked across at him and smiled.

'I'd love some.'

CHAPTER THREE

'MEG! Oh, it's lovely to see you again! Did you have a good holiday?'

Jackie gave her colleague a bear hug as soon as she saw her sitting in Helen's reception area.

The small, plump, dark-haired doctor smiled at Jackie. 'I've just been telling Helen all about it. As soon as I retire I'm going to go and live out there.'

'Retire? Steady on, Meg, you've got years to go yet.'

Jackie accepted the mug of coffee that Helen was thrusting into her hands.

'Thanks, Helen. Just what I needed.'

Meg ran a hand over her short dark hair. 'I had to get the colouring shampoo out as soon as I got home last night. Couldn't let everybody see the greying colour my hair really is when it's been ravaged by the sun and the sea. I'm planning to retire when I'm fifty so I've only got three years to go.'

Jackie took a sip of her coffee. The surgery without Meg was unthinkable! She seemed to have been here for ever. She would have to dissuade her.

'You'd get bored, Meg, if you retired so early.'

'Oh, no, I wouldn't! I'll go out to my favourite Greek island. My grandmother was Greek, you know. I speak the language so I always get a warm welcome. I'll swim and walk, and the doctor who runs the surgery out there has offered me a part-time post when I retire and go and live there.'

'Sure that's all he's offered you?' Helen said.

Meg laughed. 'Trust you to lower the tone, Helen. No, he's not my type.'

'Who is your type?' Helen persisted.

Jackie noticed there was a far-away look in Meg's eyes. She'd seen it so often before. Close friends that they were, Meg never talked about her love life—or the lack of it.

Meg smiled. 'I think Paul Newman might fit the bill.'

Jackie laughed. 'You're not fussy, are you?'

Suddenly her hand wobbled as she saw Tom coming in through the back door. Some of the coffee spilled on her clean skirt. She whispered an expletive under her breath as she put her coffee down on the counter.

Helen grabbed a tissue and dabbed at the stain.

'Better get some water on this. Why don't you take it off and button yourself into a white coat?'

'Thanks, Helen.' Jackie stood up. 'Tom, come and meet Meg,' she said in as normal a voice as possible as she fled up the stairs to her room.

She peeled off the damp skirt and started buttoning herself into a white coat. How many hours was it since Tom had held her against him? True, he'd only been comforting her and she should have moved away sooner than she had.

It didn't mean anything to him. He was a kind, caring doctor looking after someone who was feeling sad, but the touch of his lips on her cheek had been impossibly disturbing.

She knew she was overreacting. It was five years since she'd been near a man so, from a medical point of view, it was only natural that any sort of physical contact would disturb her. That's all it was—the awakening of her sensuality—and she would have to fight it all the way if it ever happened again.

Which it wouldn't! She didn't want to get involved with Tom—or any other man, for that matter! Her life was full enough, without embarking on the turmoil that a relationship would bring.

She took a deep breath as she glanced in the mirror. If she applied fresh lipstick now it would look as if she was trying too hard to make herself look attractive—and she wasn't! She licked her lips. Leave them natural. Make him think she didn't care. It was just a normal working day. But after last night...

She'd better see how Tom was getting on with Meg. There hadn't been time for a proper introduction.

Downstairs again, handing over the damp skirt for Helen's expert ministrations, she discovered that Tom and Meg were getting on like a house on fire.

'It's great to have another member of the team, isn't it, Jackie?' Tom looked at her across the reception area.

'Absolutely! It's been a real strain holding the fort without you, Meg. Things eased out when Tom joined the firm but...'

She wished he wouldn't look at her like that, with those expressive eyes. It was so unnerving when she was trying so hard to calm her feelings.

With an effort she gathered her wits about her. 'It's nice to have you back, Meg. Well, if you two can cope with morning surgery I'll make an early start on the house calls.'

'What about your skirt?' Helen was holding it out towards her. 'I've got the stain out but it's too damp to put on.'

'I'll call home and find another one.'

As she drove down the lane to the cottage she felt a distinct sense of relief. Working alongside Tom was going to be a strain—in the nicest possible way! She'd wanted to get out this morning, to sort out the emotions he'd churned up last night.

She really must try to damp down the excitement she felt whenever he came near her. People would start to talk. The disastrous coffee stain episode hadn't been lost on Helen!

It took only a couple of minutes to change her skirt and

she was back on the road. The first patient on the list was old Mrs Dunton. Her arthritis meant that she was housebound and she always welcomed Jackie's visits.

As she drove up the muddy farm track she could see Ethel Dunton, peering out through the window. Her son always settled her by the window before he went outside to work on the farm.

Jackie parked in the farmyard and breathed in the country smell. There was a definite hint of essence of pig in the air but it didn't detract from the glorious outdoor freshness. Mmm, it was good to be alive on a morning like this. She looked up at the blue sky and revelled in the feeling of the warm sun on her face.

Stepping over the dried muddy cobblestones, she tapped on the kitchen door.

'Come in, dear. It's not locked.'

Mrs Dunton beamed her welcoming smile as Jackie pushed open the door. 'The kettle's on the hob and you know where the teabags are, don't you?'

Jackie never refused the obligatory cup of tea. She remembered calling in to see Mrs Dunton with her father when she was very small. He used to take her on his house calls sometimes and she'd been plied with sweets and lemonade. Since becoming a 'proper doctor', as her patients called her, she'd graduated to tea.

'How are you feeling, Mrs Dunton?' she asked as she lifted the heavy, blackened kettle from the fire, making a mental note that Bill Dunton still hadn't bought the electric kettle she'd suggested would be less dangerous.

Summer and winter alike, Ethel Dunton's son kept the fire smouldering in the kitchen and the old kettle quietly humming to itself. Jackie didn't care to think what would happen if Ethel Dunton suddenly took it into her head to try and make herself a cup of tea.

'I'm as well as can be expected, Jackie…I mean Doctor.' The old lady grinned.

Jackie smiled back. 'Oh, come on, Mrs Dunton, there's no need to stand on ceremony with me, is there? I can remember you giving me sweets from that tin up there. The one with the picture of a rabbit on it. It seems like only yesterday so, please, let me still be Jackie to you. Now, you were saying…?'

'I can't sleep for the pain, Jackie. And these blessed hands are getting more and more useless.'

The old lady held out her gnarled, bent fingers. Jackie examined the spoon-shaped tips, wishing there was something she could do to unbend them. If only somebody could come up with a real miracle cure for arthritis!

'I'll give you some different tablets to help you sleep, and I'd like to try you on a new kind of medication to help the arthritis,' she said, opening up her medical bag.

She was well aware that she could only take palliative measures with this patient but anything that eased the pain would help, and just having someone to care about her seemed to cheer her up.

At the end of the visit, as she got back into the car, Mrs Dunton's smiling face was at the window and she was mouthing, 'Drive carefully, Jackie!'

'I will, Mrs Dunton,' she called with a smile.

As she drove off she knew that her patient would be watching until she was out of sight, still marvelling at the fact that Dr Brent's little girl had grown up to be a 'proper doctor'.

She drove round the narrow country lanes to the next village to see Babs White. The community nurse had left a message that she was worried about her.

'Not long to go now, Babs,' Jackie said, as she fixed the cuff of the sphygmomanometer around her patient's upper arm so that she could take her blood pressure.

'I'll be so glad when this baby's here, Doctor,' Babs said, leaning back in the flower patterned, cotton-covered sofa. 'I'm fed up with being as big as a house and, with these fat legs, I don't like to go out.'

Jackie examined the puffy legs and decided that she would prescribe a mild diuretic to ease the water retention. That's all it could be. She'd already checked that there were no cardiovascular problems on a previous visit. Her patient's blood pressure this time was on the high side but not dangerously so.

'Have you had any headaches, Babs?'

'No.'

'Good. I'll ask Sister Stanton to keep popping in to see you as you're finding it difficult to get in to the surgery.'

As she drove away Jackie felt that she, too, would be relieved to see this baby delivered. Some patients romped through their first pregnancy but Babs had suffered every ailment in the book. Still, her last scan had shown a healthy foetus curled up inside the uterus and there wasn't long to go now.

The other calls on her list took up the entire morning. She could have phoned in to say she was going straight home for lunch but she decided to go back to the surgery.

She wanted to see Meg again, didn't she? That was what she tried to tell herself as she pulled into the car park.

Tom was coming out of the back door as she stepped out of her car.

'Going anywhere for lunch, Jackie?'

Her heart began to pound. 'I haven't given it a thought. I was going to have a sandwich at home.'

'You wouldn't take pity on an old bachelor and make it two, would you?'

She hesitated, but only for a second as she tried to soothe her conscience. It would be churlish to deny him a sandwich after the delicious supper he'd cooked her last night, wouldn't it?

'I think my loaf might stretch to two sandwiches. Is everything OK in the surgery?'

'Running like clockwork. Leave your car here. We'll take mine.'

His large, shiny, steel-grey car seemed to swamp her small semi-circular driveway. She was glad she hadn't any immediate neighbours to notice that she was entertaining in her lunch hour. Thank goodness the girls were at school!

'It's a lovely house,' Tom said, standing back to admire it as she fiddled with the doorkey.

'It used to be three cottages in the sixteenth century before it was made into one house. It had a thatched roof until the beginning of this century, I believe. The tiles are more practicable.'

'And they don't detract from its chocolate-box image,' he said. 'I like the roses round the door. Very picturesque!'

She smiled, pleased that he approved of her house. His opinion mattered a great deal to her. 'Come in.'

She took him through the kitchen to the little breakfast room. He sat down at the oval, nineteenth-century oak table and looked around at the framed photographs on the walls.

'That's where we keep all the family portraits,' she said, plugging in the kettle and rinsing out the teapot.

She carried the bread board to the table and began slicing the fresh granary loaf she'd bought in the village shop on the way back from her rounds.

'I hope you like doorstep sandwiches.'

He smiled. 'I do when it's good old-fashioned bread like that.'

She topped the slices with ham, before handing him the mustard, a tomato and a jar of gherkins.

'Another cup of tea?' she asked, as he finished the last crumb on his plate.

'Yes, please.'

He leaned back against the ancient settle, running his hands over the gnarled, indented oak arms.

'This is an interesting piece of furniture. Is it very old?'

'Yes, but I don't know the exact date. My father bought it from a pub that was closing down, but I believe it came from a church originally. It's had a lot of wear and tear over the years so it definitely didn't need to be distressed artificially like some of the reproduction pieces.'

He was watching her thoughtfully, his eyes appraising her enthusiasm.

'You obviously like antiques. So do I. We could go round some of the antique shops in this area. I could check out the paintings and you could add to your collection.'

'I'd like that,' she said. It couldn't do any harm to go prowling around looking at antiques, could it?

He was looking up at the photographs on the wall again. 'Is that David?'

She nodded as he stood up to get a better view of the fair-haired man, holding the twins on his lap.

'He looks older than I imagined.' He sat down again.

'He was twelve years older than me. He was thirty when he joined my father's practice. I was only eighteen. We fell in love, even though there was such a big age difference. It was difficult to see each other because I'd just started at medical school in London and couldn't get home very often. But David wanted us to get married. He persuaded my parents that marriage wouldn't interfere with my career.'

'And how did you feel about that?'

She looked at him in surprise. 'I wanted it, too... Well, I think I would have preferred to wait but I was so much in love with David that I didn't want to lose him.'

She took another sip of her tea. 'He could be very persuasive when he wanted his own way. It was David's idea that we start a family as soon as possible.'

'But that must have been very difficult for you, with your medical studies only just started.'

The memories came flooding back. 'It was. I became pregnant two months after the wedding. The twins were born when I was just nineteen. I took a year off to be with them and when I resumed my studies my mother took care of them when I couldn't be here.'

'Did you all live in this house?'

'Yes. It was convenient for the surgery and my parents liked having the girls living with them. We planned to buy our own house when the girls were older, but that didn't happen. They were eleven when David died. We'd started looking at houses but...David was very fussy and we hadn't found anything suitable.'

She paused, leaning back in her chair as the memories flooded back.

'After David died I was in such a state of shock that it was a good thing the girls and I were still living with my parents. They helped me pull through the initial trauma.'

'How soon after David's death did you lose your parents?' he asked gently, in a sympathetic tone of voice.

She swallowed hard. 'It was just over a year.'

He reached out and took hold of her hand. 'You've had a difficult time. It must be hard to forget the past.'

'It is.'

'But you've got to try really hard, Jackie. You've got to move on,' he said evenly.

She glanced at him, but his eyes were giving nothing away.

She removed her hand from his clasp. 'I'm perfectly happy with my life as it is,' she said quickly. 'I've come to terms with the situation.'

'Have you?' he asked quietly.

'Yes, I think so.'

Neither of them spoke for a while but the silence wasn't

uncomfortable. Jackie felt sure that Tom was thinking about what she'd told him. She'd never felt so at ease with anyone when she was talking about the past.

She glanced up at the kitchen clock and was surprised to see how the time had flown.

'I think I should be getting back to the surgery. It's the mother and baby clinic this afternoon and...'

He stood up and came round the table, holding out his arms towards her. She hesitated for a fraction of a second before allowing herself to experience his comforting embrace as she leaned her head against his shoulder. For a few seconds they remained like that, neither of them speaking.

'Don't hide yourself away in your work, Jackie.'

She pulled herself away. 'I'm not hiding myself in my work. The fact is I have to go to the clinic and—'

'Sister Saunders is perfectly capable of running the clinic, and Helen will be fussing around like a mother hen. Let's take a couple of hours off and prowl round the antique shops. We won't go far and they can speak to you on the mobile if there's a problem. What do you say?'

'Sounds very tempting,' she said slowly.

He grinned. 'So why not give in to temptation for once?'

She could feel the excitement rising inside her. How long had it been since she'd felt like this, as if she wanted to go out and enjoy herself?

She smiled. 'OK, you're on.'

She picked up the phone before she could change her mind. Rosemary Saunders was perfectly happy about the arrangement, promising to call Jackie if she had a problem she couldn't handle, but added that it was highly unlikely.

Tom stood up. 'So, we've got the whole afternoon ahead of us. I've drawn up a list of some of the shops we could visit.'

She laughed, a delicious sense of abandonment creeping over her. 'So this little expedition was planned, was it?'

'Of course it was planned. Not necessarily for this afternoon, but for some time soon. Let's go!'

'Give me a minute to change. I need to put on something cooler than this thick skirt and blouse.'

She ran upstairs and pulled out the wildly outrageous Bali dress. 'Yes, Cinderella, you shall go to the ball,' she whispered to her reflection in the mirror.

The years seemed to have dropped away from her. She was young again, full of hope for the future. Saying yes to Tom had been a milestone. Oh, it was only a tour of stuffy old antique shops, for heaven's sake, but it meant she would be seen out in public with a man, even if he was only her medical colleague.

Her hair didn't go with the dress! She dragged out the pins from the chignon and brushed vigorously. Thank goodness her hair was freshly washed in the shower this morning! The sun, streaming through the window, was giving highlights to the dark, shining strands. But it was too long to wear over her shoulders. She looked like a teenager—until you noticed the creases on her forehead and the deep-set crinkles round her eyes!

She searched in her drawer. Somewhere, among all this junk she was planning to sort out, there was…ah, there it was! A dear little elastic band covered in black cotton. It had come out of a Christmas cracker and she'd stashed it away, thinking that one day it might come in useful.

Pulling her hair back over her shoulders she twined the band around it to create a sort of modified pony-tail. She pulled a few strands of hair forward over her forehead to soften the effect, before tripping lightly out on to the landing.

Downstairs, she discovered that Tom had cleared the table, put the plates and mugs in the dishwasher and was studiously wiping away the crumbs that had fallen on the floor. He stood up from his crouching position and whistled.

'Wow, you look nice!'

'Thanks!' She felt nice. In fact, she felt like a completely new woman!

Outside in the car he switched off the air-conditioning because Jackie said she preferred the fresh air. She pressed the automatic button and the window shot down.

As Tom drove along the narrow, country lanes she breathed in the fresh air and allowed the breeze to ruffle her hair.

'My mobile phone is being considerately silent, Tom.'

'Relax! Sister Saunders is one of the most competent gynae and obstetrics sisters I've ever come across. And if there's an emergency Helen will handle it.'

Jackie smiled. 'Helen assisted me once with a premature delivery because there was no one else around.'

'Well, there you are, then! You've got a brilliant team. Why not enjoy yourself?'

He took one hand from the steering-wheel and placed it over hers. The touch of his fingers was unsettling her. Was this going too far? Allowing herself to hold hands as they drove along was very forward but she couldn't pull her hand away now. Besides, it gave her such a warm feeling of companionship.

Companionship—that's all it was. She wasn't going to allow herself to go any further.

Tom stopped outside a barn conversion in the next village. A middle-aged man with grey hair looked up from the books he was dusting and smiled when they walked in to his high-ceilinged building.

Jackie glanced up at the rafters and saw a sparrow, perched on an old oak beam. Below, on top of a pile of *Tatler* magazines, a sleek black cat was crouching hopefully, ready to pounce if the twittering bird should come down low enough.

'Can I help you?' The man came towards them.

Tom smiled. 'We'd like to browse around. You look as if you've got some interesting pieces.'

'What exactly are you looking for?'

'Nothing in particular,' Jackie said quickly. 'Just looking.'

They wandered for a while amid the old furniture. There were tables, chairs, wardrobes and ancient chests. Tom became interested in an old mariner's chest with brass handles.

The owner came across to rouse his interest further. 'It belonged to a ship's captain, sir. Early nineteenth century. See where the salt has worked its way into the wood. A very fine example.'

As the men started to discuss the price Jackie went over to look at a table of small bric-à-brac. There were some delightful little silver thimbles that the girls would like for their collection. She selected two and went back to see how the financial negotiations were going on.

The men were shaking hands and smiling. Obviously, a mutual agreement had been reached. She asked how much the thimbles were and the owner said he would give her a special price. It seemed a reasonable sum so she said she would take them.

'Do you collect thimbles?' he asked, wrapping them in tissue paper.

'They're for my daughters.'

She put her shoulder-bag on the owner's desk and pulled out her wallet.

Tom was handing over a cheque. The man glanced at it and smiled. 'The thimbles are paid for, madam. Your husband...I mean, the gentleman has included them in his cheque.'

Jackie looked up at Tom. 'You must let me pay you back.'

He was smiling down at her, his expressive eyes twinkling. 'I'd like to give the girls a present.'

'Yes, but...' She stopped, aware that the owner was listening to every word. Better not make a fuss in here.

The sparrow up above them had stopped taunting the cat and was winging its way to freedom through the open barn doors. The cat leapt in the air, howling with frustration, but the bird was too swift for it.

'Thank you,' she said quietly, as she turned and followed the bird out into the bright sunlight.

The owner shook hands with them at the door. 'Do come again. It's been a pleasure to do business with you.'

Tom picked up the chest and carried it out, carefully securing it in the boot of the car. It was too tall, so the owner helped him to fasten it in place with a piece of rope.

As soon as they had driven away Jackie turned to speak to Tom.

'It was very kind of you to buy the thimbles for the girls but I really would rather pay for them myself. They might think, well, they might misconstrue...'

'You mean they might think I'm trying to buy their approval,' he said evenly.

She hesitated, searching for the right words so that she wouldn't hurt his feelings.

'I haven't been out with a man since their father died, and I'm not sure how they'll take it. They may feel...' She paused, finding it difficult to express herself.

'You mean they may feel I'm trying to take over from their father?'

'Yes...I mean, no. Oh...'

He laughed. 'I know what you're trying to say, Jackie, but don't worry about it. I'm not muscling in on your little domain. I think the girls will accept the thimbles for what they are, a couple of simple little presents.'

'It's very kind of you,' she said, still secretly worried that Tom's generous gesture might be misconstrued.

She looked out of the car window. They were passing a field of strawberries. A bold sign read, PICK YOUR OWN STRAWBERRIES, FIRST CROP OF THE SEASON.

Tom slowed down and pulled into the farmyard.

'Tom, we haven't time to pick strawberries.'

He grinned. 'No, but we've time to eat a few.'

She followed him over the grass to a small paved area in front of the farm shop where wooden tables, shaded by colourful umbrellas, had been placed.

He smiled down at her. 'Do you take cream with your strawberries, madame?'

She laughed at his impersonation of a waiter. 'Yes, please.'

He went into the shop and returned to their table with two dishes of freshly picked strawberries, a jug of cream, a pot of tea and two cups and saucers.

Jackie put down her spoon as she finished the last strawberry. 'Delicious!'

He reached across and took hold of her hand. 'I think I've had enough antique-hunting for this afternoon. Let's take a walk down by the river.'

They left the car in the farmyard and followed the path down between fields of strawberries to an ancient mill, complete with water wheel. Upstream from the mill was a miniature lake. They stood leaning on the bridge, watching the ducks and swans swimming around.

Leaning over the parapet of the bridge, Jackie could see their reflections in the smooth water below, as clear as a looking-glass. She liked what she saw—a man and a woman together. Friends—they were just good friends, she told herself firmly.

They walked along the side of the river. It seemed perfectly natural that Tom should hold her hand in his so she didn't resist when his fingers closed around hers. There was no pressure of his fingers, no intimation that he was stirred in a sensual way. But it felt just so...so right somehow, even though she was desperately trying to ignore the sensuously warm, tingling feeling that was gravitating up her arm.

After a few minutes, she said, 'I think we ought to turn back now.'

He smiled down at her. 'Let's not go back just yet. It's so peaceful out here.'

Then he bent his head and kissed her on the lips. With a pang of guilt she felt herself responding. As his kiss deepened she knew she wanted more. On the one hand she felt relieved that her senses were normal after all this time, but on the other she knew she mustn't surrender to this deep-down, treacherous feeling of sensuality.

His hands were caressing her, holding her against him in a breathtaking embrace. She could feel shivers of desire running down her spine.

She moved out of his arms and stepped backwards, breathing deeply. 'I think we should be getting back to the surgery.'

She saw his eyes flicker and heard the sharp, impatient intake of his breath. He seemed about to make a retort as he struggled to calm himself but, in the end, he remained silent.

She knew she should have moved out of his embrace sooner. She should have discouraged his advances, she should... But she'd been experiencing such wonderful feelings. It had been so hard to tear herself away.

He didn't try to hold her hand on the way back to the car but she could feel the electric tension pulsating between them. Settling back in her seat, she said she'd better call the surgery and check if she was needed.

'They would have phoned if there was a problem,' Tom said evenly.

He started the engine and drove out of the farmyard back onto the road. Jackie punched in the surgery digits and waited for someone to answer.

Helen seemed surprised to hear Jackie's voice.

'Yes, of course we're OK. I'm just about to do my strong-arm bouncer act and eject the stragglers who don't seem to have any homes to go to but apart from that, it's been a successful afternoon. Who's doing evening surgery?'

'I am.' Tom, negotiating the narrow country lane, had been able to hear every word of the conversation.

'Tom's going to take it, Helen. Goodbye.'

She turned to look at Tom, whose eyes were studiously on the road. 'I wish you hadn't spoken just now. Helen will know we've been out together.'

'And is that so bad?' he said tersely. 'Hunting for antiques, enjoying a cream tea, walking by the river?'

She remained silent. When it was described like that it did seem fairly innocuous. Maybe she was reading more into the situation than actually existed.

She came to a decision. 'I'd like to pay you for the thimbles,' she said firmly, taking out her cheque-book.

'If you insist,' he said, his tone barely concealing his impatience.

She scribbled a cheque and put it in the pocket of his jacket. He continued to look straight ahead, his face an enigmatic mask.

She could feel the tension that had risen between them. Minutes elapsed when neither of them spoke and then Tom broke the silence. His calm, even tone showed that he was completely in control of the situation.

'It's hardly worth me going all the way back to Estersea before evening surgery,' he said. 'I suppose you wouldn't offer me a cup of tea at your place?'

She hesitated, unsure how the girls would react when they heard she'd spent the afternoon with Tom. Well, maybe she should find out!

'I'd love to give you a cup of tea,' she said quickly.

Tom pulled into the drive and parked the car. She took her key from her bag, but as she approached the front door and went to put it in the lock the door opened.

'Hi, Mum! Where've you been?' Fiona said.

'Antique-hunting.'

She turned to look at Tom, who was standing right behind her.

'You remember Dr Prestwick?'

'How do you do, sir?' Fiona said, in a polite voice.

'Oh, please, call me Tom.'

Fiona went into the kitchen. Jackie followed her. Debbie was seated in the breakfast alcove, eating toast and peanut-butter.

'Hi, Mum.'

Jackie was painfully aware that her daughters were scrutinising her way-out dress and the new hairstyle.

'Did you wear that dress in the surgery today, Mum?' Fiona asked.

'No, I changed into it this afternoon,' Jackie said in a measured tone. 'Why do you ask?'

'Because...I don't like it,' Fiona said. 'It makes you look—'

'Did I hear you say you've been antique-hunting?' Debbie interrupted quickly. 'Buy anything nice?'

'As a matter of fact, I did.'

She handed over the two small packets.

'Oh, that's beautiful, Mum!' Debbie said, kissing her mother on the cheek and placing the thimble on her little finger. 'Thanks a lot.'

'Thanks, Mum, that's great!' Fiona said, kissing Jackie's other cheek. 'How many have we got now, Debbie?'

'Let's go and check.' The girls dashed off upstairs to inspect their collection.

'Well, now, how about that cup of tea?' Jackie said, filling the kettle. 'And maybe some toast and peanut-butter?'

Tom settled himself at the table. 'No, thanks, to the peanut-butter but I'd love a cup a tea.'

Jackie could hear the girls chattering excitedly upstairs as she sipped her tea.

For a few minutes they made polite conversation, during

which Jackie was very much aware that Tom was watching her across the table. Suddenly he put down his cup. 'The girls seem happy with their presents,' he said evenly. 'Do you really think they would have resented me buying them?'

'I can't be sure,' she said quickly. 'I haven't brought a man to the house before and...'

His expressive brown eyes flickered. 'And you don't want them to think I'm planning to usurp their idolised father. Is that what you're trying to say?'

She swallowed. 'Something like that.'

'I think you're worrying about it more than they are, Jackie,' he said, standing up. 'Thanks for the tea.'

She hovered on the threshold, watching him go out to his car. They were two polite friends again.

She closed her eyes and leaned against the door after he'd gone.

'Mum, are you all right?' Debbie said, coming up silently in her bare feet.

Jackie snapped open her eyes. 'Yes, I'm fine.'

Fiona was following close behind. 'Are you going to go out with him again?' she asked.

'I don't know,' Jackie said, her heart pounding as she went back into the kitchen and sat at the table. The girls joined her.

'Do you fancy him?' Fiona asked, picking up a piece of toast and spreading it, thickly, with peanut-butter.

'I enjoy going out with him,' Jackie said carefully.

'Do you think he fancies you?' Debbie asked.

'I've no idea,' Jackie said. 'We're just good friends.'

Fiona smiled. 'I'm glad about that because nobody could ever replace Dad, could they? You wouldn't want somebody else, would you, Mum?'

She swallowed hard. 'No, of course not,' she said quickly. 'Now, what shall we cook for supper, or have you two filled yourselves up with too much tea?'

CHAPTER FOUR

JACKIE sat at her desk, opening the morning post which Helen had stacked in a neat pile. As she slit open the official-looking envelope her thoughts turned, unwillingly, to Tom.

He'd suggested lunch yesterday and she'd made a flimsy, spur-of-the-moment excuse. He'd appeared on the surface to accept it, but she remembered the expression in his eyes and knew that he hadn't been fooled.

It was a week since their afternoon out, browsing in the antiques shop and wandering along beside the river, and she was still trying to come to terms with her churning emotions. She couldn't go out with Tom again until she could handle the situation better. She was trying to convince herself that she simply wanted a friend, not...

She sighed as she looked down at the piece of paper she'd extricated from the envelope—she had to concentrate.

The letter was from the regional health authority, outlining the facilities now available at the new Estersea medical centre. There was a section which would be of interest to Tom.

She pressed the intercom, took a deep breath and put on her professional voice.

'Are you busy, Tom? Could you come in here for a minute?'

'I'm on my way.'

She ran a hand through her hair. She'd washed it in the shower that morning and it was flying all over the place.

The door opened.

'Just got this letter and thought we should confer.'

Tom closed the door behind him and moved over to settle in the chair in front of her desk. She watched as he sat down,

hitching up the cloth from the knees of his trousers and un-
buttoning his jacket. His suit was a subtle shade of blue. He
put one hand on the desk and looked across at her, his brown
eyes alive with interest.

'It's about the Estersea centre, isn't it? I've got a letter,
too. It seems an excellent idea.'

She hesitated. 'I like the idea of them being able to provide
minor surgery at the centre. That's going to help reduce the
waiting lists at the hospital. It's this bit...'

She glanced down at the letter and began to read out loud.

'General practitioners in the area will be welcome to
come and observe surgical procedures, especially those involving their own patients. Trained and experienced surgeons will be invited to work for half a day at the centre
on a regular basis. Dr Tom Prestwick, who is currently
working in your practice, would fall into this category
and—'

'Yes, I know all this, and I'd like to spend one afternoon
a week doing surgery.' He smiled. 'That is, unless you've
any objections?'

'No, I've no objections so long as it doesn't affect the
smooth running of the practice.'

'Well, that's settled, then.' He stood. 'I'll give them a call
and fix a date.'

His tone was as brisk as hers had been curt. They were
two professionals, embarking on a new venture. She had the
vague feeling that her authority was being undermined. Tom
had never been cut out to play second fiddle!

He turned at the door and looked directly across at her.

'I'll let you know what they say.'

Minutes later he was back, his eyes glowing with enthusiasm.

'They want me to start next week. Thursday afternoon.'

'But that's your half-day.'

He smiled. 'I know, but I wasn't going anywhere.'

'Fine, if you're happy with the arrangement. I'll try and fix you up with some more off-duty when I can.'

'Don't worry about it. I'll enjoy an afternoon in the operating theatre. Will you come down to observe?'

She hesitated. 'If I'm free and if any of our patients are involved.'

The following Thursday Tom drove her down to the Estersea medical centre. Once inside the shiny, new reception area a couple of white-uniformed nurses were assigned to escort them.

Jackie saw Tom being taken away to the theatre scrub room, while she was assigned to the observation area—a series of seats on wide, raised steps which ran along a whole wall of the operating theatre. She was impressed with the design.

Looking down from her second-row seat, she had an excellent view of the operating table. A couple of theatre nurses were setting out the sterile instruments.

She hadn't observed like this since her student days. It seemed unreal somehow. More like going to a non-surgical theatre to see a show. She'd even been given a list of the patients, set out like a programme, in the order in which they were going to be operated on.

One of her patients was number one on the list. She'd told everybody that was the reason she was here, but she knew she would have come anyway just to see Tom operate.

She waited and watched. The observation rows were filling up—a group of medical students came in together and sat nearby. She recognised a colleague from a neighbouring practice and smiled across.

The surgical team were assembling. The unconscious patient was wheeled in and the buzz of conversation died.

Tom took his place at the side of the patient, before look-ing up at the students and explaining that he was going to perform a dilatation and curettage.

'Diane Grainger is twenty-seven, no children and suffering from heavy periods and occasional cramp-like abdominal pains.' He was now looking down and concentrating on their patient again.

Jackie remembered Diane coming in to see her a few weeks ago, tearful and fed-up with herself. She'd complained that she and her husband were desperate for a baby but all she got was heavy periods and tummy-ache. Jackie had put her on the hospital waiting list for a D and C and now, with the advent of the new centre, she was getting her operation sooner than expected.

'I'm introducing graduated dilators to open the neck of the womb wide enough for me to introduce a sponge-holding forceps,' Tom explained for the benefit of the students.

'I'm checking out the lining of the womb now…and, yes, there we are! That was the culprit.'

Tom held up a large endometrial polyp, clamped between his forceps.

His eyes met Jackie's as she breathed a sigh of relief. With a now-healthy womb, her patient stood a good chance of having that long-desired baby. She smiled down at Tom and his eyes above the mask were smiling in answer.

As Diane Grainger was being wheeled out Jackie saw the theatre sister, who had been called away, return to speak urgently with Tom. She saw him nodding.

'No problem, Sister,' she heard him say.

He was looking up at the students again. 'We're going to bring in an emergency patient, ladies and gentlemen. Appar-ently, there's a blockage on the road which leads from Estersea to the main Colchester road. Those of you who are familiar with the area will know that it's the only road. Apparently, an oil tanker has overturned on a narrow bend.

The driver isn't hurt but an ambulance, following only yards behind, has had to turn back to Estersea and bring the patient here.'

As he spoke the swing doors were opening to admit the unconscious patient.

Jackie found herself admiring the calm way in which Tom was dealing with the unexpected turn of events. She felt proud that he was with her practice. And she also felt something else, which had nothing to do with pride and was infinitely more disturbing.

She looked down towards the operating table, concentrating all her thoughts on the patient.

Tom was explaining that Sally, their patient, had gone into labour a short time ago. She was thirty-six weeks pregnant, four weeks before full term. Her GP had discovered, early on in the pregnancy, that her pelvis was too small to allow the passage of the foetal head.

'So, because Sally's doctor had diagnosed that she was suffering from cephalopelvic disproportion, he'd booked her into Colchester General for a Caesarean. The baby decided it wanted to make an early appearance and the ambulance couldn't get through so, not having time to scramble a helicopter...'

All the time he was talking he was working on the patient.

'As you can see, I've cut through the abdominal wall and now I'm going to make an incision into the lower segment of the uterus, and soon...'

Jackie could see the lines of concentration on his usually unwrinkled brow. Theatre Sister had leaned across to wipe away a trickle of sweat that threatened to drop down. The lights were bright and very hot.

As Tom extricated a tiny infant from the depths of the patient's uterus there was a collective sigh of relief.

'As you can all see, it's a boy!' Tom said.

The infant made a loud wail as Tom held him up to the admiring observers.

Jackie watched as Tom handed the baby to Sister, before concentrating once more on the internal organs of the patient. When he was fully satisfied with the state of the uterus he began the task of internal and external suturing.

There still remained the long list of routine surgery, but Tom accomplished it in the same calm, skilful manner. Jackie knew she was impressed—she was more than impressed.

It was early evening before the list was finished. She was invited into the staff common room for a cup of tea. She drank it quickly, glancing at her watch. It was her turn to do evening surgery.

'Do you know if the road has been cleared yet?' she asked Theatre Sister.

She was told that the tanker had just been successfully removed but that there was a long line of traffic.

'I'd better go,' Jackie said to Tom. 'I should have brought my car.'

'I told you, I've got to go into Colchester,' he said. 'I'll drop you off at the surgery.'

Minutes later, sitting in the traffic jam on the narrow road, Jackie extricated her mobile from the depths of her bag.

'I'd better phone Meg and see if she's free to start the surgery, otherwise—'

'Don't panic! It should clear soon—look, we're moving.'

She leaned back against the seat.

'I could help you out with the evening surgery and then we could go out for a meal together,' he said evenly.

She felt the increase of her pulse. 'I thought you had an engagement this evening.'

He smiled. 'I'm only going to check out a restaurant that I've read about in the *Good Food Guide*.'

It sounded very tempting, but wasn't this the sort of situation she was trying to avoid? Going out in the evening with Tom would be just too...

'Not tonight, Tom. I'd prefer to get back to the girls. I usually see them at teatime but today—'

'I know, I know,' he said.

She heard his impatient tone. He was recognising that she was a hopeless case, that she was never going to go out with him in the evening. Well, that was what she wanted—wasn't it?

A couple of minutes of silence elapsed before he spoke again.

'A little bird told me it's your birthday next week,' he said, his voice agreeably whimsical again.

'So?' She held her breath.

'So, I think you should break your self-imposed rules and let me take you out. I'm giving you lots of warning so you can make all the necessary arrangements to your complicated domestic schedule. If I like this restaurant tonight I'll make a booking for next week. What do you say?'

She drew in her breath as she tried to calm her churning emotions. 'Well, put like that, how can I refuse?'

He laughed. 'How indeed!'

On the morning of her birthday Jackie's apprehensive excitement about her date with Tom had reached fever pitch.

'And now, about tonight,' she began briskly, as she stood up to leave the breakfast table.

Fiona and Deborah looked up from their cornflake bowls and eyed her warily. Jackie suppressed a sigh as she tried to remain positive about her intentions.

The morning had started well, with presents and birthday cards to open, hugs and kisses and the ritual singing of 'Happy Birthday'. It had been just like the old days when the girls had believed she knew the answers to everything in the world.

Fiona put down her spoon. 'Are you really going out with Dr Prestwick again, Mum?'

'Fiona, in the five weeks I've known Tom Prestwick I've been out with him twice. Once to his house for supper and once to look at antique shops.'

'Well, I suppose you know what you're doing,' Fiona said quietly, as she resumed eating her breakfast.

Jackie drew in her breath. If only! Three weeks on from the afternoon she'd spent with Tom, she knew she'd been very careful about her relationship with him. In fact, there hadn't been a relationship at all. Apart from working with him at the surgery and observing him in the operating theatre last week, she hadn't seen him.

Debbie looked up from her cornflakes and smiled at Jackie. 'You know, it's probably a good idea for you to get out occasionally, Mum. You work very hard.'

Jackie smiled. 'Thanks, Debbie. Now, about tonight. Meg's coming for tea so that's when we'll have the birthday cake.'

'Great!' Fiona said. 'Is she going to stay the night?'

'She may do. She hadn't decided when I asked her yesterday. But she knows the guest room is always ready for her. I've got to get ready for work now.'

As she ran up the stairs she thought how much the girls loved her friend and colleague. Meg had been like a surrogate aunt to them since David died.

'Happy birthday to you,' sang Helen and Meg as she walked through the back door of the surgery into the reception area. 'Happy birthday, dear Jackie, happy birthday to you!'

'Thanks.' Jackie could feel her cheeks glowing as she stood in the doorway, listening to the serenade, because Tom had been only a few steps behind her as she came from the car park.

She could tell he'd caught up with her as she felt his warm breath on the back of her neck.

'Happy birthday, Jackie.'

He was looking down at her, his expression warm and tender. She hoped no one else could see it.

'Thanks.'

'Come and open your prezzie,' Helen called.

Helen had bought her a bone china hedgehog to add to her animal collection.

'Oh, it's beautiful. Thank you very much, Helen!'

Meg's present was an antique, leather-bound book of poetry. There were more thanks, more hugs.

'Where's Tom?' Helen said, looking around the reception area.

'He's gone upstairs,' Meg said. 'I expect he's saving his present till later.'

Helen gave Jackie a knowing smile. 'You two seeing each other later, then, Jackie?'

'Tom's taking me out for supper,' she said, escaping up the stairs to her room before she had to answer any more questions.

Tom was standing looking out of the window, the bright morning sunshine illuminating his face. He turned to look at her.

'I hope you don't mind me coming in but I wanted to see you alone.' He moved towards her. 'Happy birthday, Jackie! Is everything OK for tonight?'

She nodded. 'Meg's coming to tea and she'll probably stay for a while—maybe all night. She gets on with the girls like a house on fire so they'll all have a fun evening.'

His eyes crinkled at the corners. 'So you've got nothing to worry about concerning the girls. Why do I have a feeling that you're the one who's unwilling to dig yourself out of a rut?'

The intercom was buzzing. 'Jackie, I've got Sister Stanton on the phone. Sounds urgent.'

'Put her through, Helen.' Jackie picked up the phone, relieved that she didn't have to answer Tom's question.

'Yes, Heather, what's the problem?'

She listened apprehensively. Heather Stanton, their community nurse, was a well-respected, experienced woman in her mid-forties. There was rarely anything she couldn't handle by herself.

'I'm worried about Babs White, Jackie. She's gone into labour but she refuses to be taken into hospital. I think it could be a difficult delivery and I don't want to take the responsibility of it myself. She says she wants to see you.'

'I'm on my way.'

'Thanks, Jackie.'

She heard the relief in Heather's voice as she put the phone down. She looked up at Tom.

'We've got a difficult obstetrics patient out at Crossways village. She should be going into hospital but—'

'I heard,' he cut in. 'Want me to come with you?'

She nodded. 'Thanks.'

As she gathered up her medical bag she felt a sense of relief that she would have an experienced obstetrician with her. If Babs refused to be taken into hospital—which she probably would, knowing how stubborn she was—Tom would be a great help with the delivery.

As Tom drove along the narrow country lanes he asked Jackie to fill him in on the case history of their patient.

'I last saw Babs a couple of weeks ago. I went out to see her because Heather had said she was worried about her and asked me to call in. Babs seemed fairly cheerful, but longing to get the delivery over. It's her first baby and she's now thirty-eight weeks so if it's on its way it should be viable.'

'How has the pregnancy been?' Tom took his eyes from the road momentarily to glance at her.

'Not easy. Babs started off with persistent morning sickness until about six months. I tried all the usual medication but nothing seemed to work. At six months I thought we were out of the woods and then she developed cystitis. It took three weeks to clear that and then we had to deal with a couple of weeks of constipation. I persuaded her to change her diet and as soon as she added lots of fruit, green vegetables and roughage the problem cleared up.'

'So nothing seriously wrong with her, I gather.'

Jackie hesitated. 'She's been a difficult patient to handle. For a start, she refuses to leave the house because her legs are swollen.'

'A good walk would probably do her good, unless— You've checked her cardiovascular system, I presume?'

'Of course. Her circulation is normal and there's nothing wrong with her heart. She's basically as strong as an ox. I agree with you that a good walk would probably work wonders but Babs is very self-conscious—says she feels as big as a house. I prescribed a mild diuretic to get rid of any water retention, which I thought would ease the problem.'

Tom was reducing speed. 'This is her road, isn't it? Is that the house?'

'Yes, the one with the brown shutters. She likes to close herself in at night because she lives on her own. Her boyfriend left her when she told him she was pregnant.'

'Oh, dear! No wonder she's difficult. Can't have been easy for her.' Tom pulled up in front of the house.

It was the middle one in a row of five, the doors opening straight out onto the country lane.

'Thank goodness you're here!' Heather Stanton said quietly, as she opened the door. 'Babs is upstairs in her bedroom, refusing to go anywhere until she's seen you, Jackie.'

'There's probably no reason why she should be moved,' Tom said, running up the stairs.

'Who's that?' Heather looked thoroughly put out.

'That's Tom Prestwick, our new doctor. He specialised in obstetrics before he came out here.'

'Well, let's hope he can sort Babs out because she's being really difficult.'

Jackie followed Heather up the stairs to find Tom sitting on the side of the bed, trying to soothe their patient who was sobbing hysterically.

'I'm not going, you know! I'm not having all those other women looking at me and pitying me because Ted ran off. They all know about it, you know. And what do I look like?'

'Nobody looks their best when they're having a baby, Babs,' Tom said in a soothing tone. 'Now, if you'll let me have a look at what's going on I may be able to let you stay here.'

The crying stopped. 'Do you really mean that, Doctor?'

Tom pursed his lips, his face deadly serious. 'That depends on what I find, Babs. I'll let you know in a few minutes.'

Heather pulled back the sheets and removed pillows so that Babs could lie flat.

'What do you think I should do, Dr Brent?' Babs asked in a tiny voice, as she reached out her hand towards Jackie.

Jackie took Babs's hand and sat down on the edge of the bed, gently stroking her patient's fingers as she used to do with the twins when they were tiny and became upset about something.

'Let's see what Dr Prestwick thinks, Babs. He's a very experienced doctor, you know. He's delivered hundreds of babies so if he thinks it's safe for you to stay here that's what we'll do.'

Babs smiled.

'Otherwise—' Jackie began, but didn't finish her sentence as she watched her patient's smile disappear. Tears were appearing once more in her eyes, threatening to erupt any second.

Tom was finishing his internal examination. He stood up

and returned to the head of the bed, a confident expression on his face.

'There's no cause for concern, Babs. Both you and the baby are very healthy so you can stay here—'

'Oh, thank you, Doctor!'

'But you'll have to cooperate fully with me,' he said firmly.

Babs nodded vigorously. 'Oh, I will. Ouch! There's another pain coming, Doctor...'

'Breathe deeply, Babs,' Jackie said in a calm voice. 'Would you like me to give you something for the pain?'

'Yes, please,' Babs said, through clenched teeth.

Jackie injected 100 mg of pethidine hydrochloride. Babs reached for Tom's hand and clung to it tightly. As the contraction subsided Jackie made Babs comfortable again, plumping up her pillows. Tom told their patient he would be back in a moment and, signalled to Jackie and Heather to follow him outside onto the landing. Babs was lying back against the pillows, her eyes closing as the pethidine began to take effect. Leaning against the banisters, Tom spoke quietly about his decision to keep Babs at home.

'I've had to weigh up the pros and cons carefully. To move her to hospital in her present state would send her into hysterics. We could control that with drugs, of course, but it would be an experience she would never forget and I, personally, think it would be detrimental to her well-being.'

'Has the baby turned?' Heather asked.

Jackie felt a shiver of apprehension. 'You mean, it's a breech presentation?'

'Yes, I'm going to try and turn it,' Tom said evenly.

'Supposing you're not successful?' Heather asked.

'I've delivered babies in breech presentation before,' Tom said in a calm voice, 'and never lost one.'

'How far on is she?' Jackie asked.

'The cervix has begun to dilate but it could take a while.

I'll go and see if I can do a successful cephalic version before
we get any further advanced. If I can get the foetal head to
present we'll have no problem.'

Jackie put her hand on Tom's arm. 'Just one thing before
you start, Tom. If it's going to be a long birth I think I should
leave you and Heather and get back to the surgery. There's
a long list of patients for Meg to cope with on her own.'

'I think it would upset Babs if you went, Jackie,' Heather
put in quickly. 'She's got a lot of faith in you.'

'And I'd like you to stay,' Tom said, his expressive eyes
searching her face. 'Why not phone Meg and assess the situation? Helen could call some of the later patients and postpone
their appointments.'

Jackie's call to the surgery revealed that Helen and Meg
had everything under control. She was told not to worry but
to make sure Babs had a safe delivery.

Tom's cephalic version was successful. With his careful,
experienced hands on Babs's abdomen, he turned the baby
round so that the head was now presenting.

But minutes later Babs cried out, putting her hands over
her tummy. 'The little blighter's playing football! Just feel
that, Doctor.'

Jackie placed her hands on Babs's abdomen. As she'd
feared, the baby had turned back again. Going out onto the
landing for a further consultation, she quietly told Tom that
the baby had decided it didn't want to dive head first after
all.

'Then we'll go ahead with the breech delivery,' he said
softly. 'This is one very stubborn baby—a chip off the old
block, don't you think?'

Jackie smiled. In spite of her apprehension, she had every
confidence in Tom.

It was late afternoon before Babs reached the final stage of
labour. Her waters had broken during the morning and the

birth passage had continued to slowly dilate. Tom had succeeded in rigging up the portable Entonox machine that he'd carried in the boot of his car, and Jackie had taught Babs how to breathe into it to relieve the pain of the contractions.

'Not long now, Babs,' Tom said, as he watched Heather swabbing the vulval and perineal areas with Hibitane 1 in 1000, the antiseptic solution he always used for deliveries.

Jackie stood beside him at the foot of the bed as he put his sterile gloved hand inside the birth canal. As she watched she saw he was holding the baby's leg. She held her breath. This was the crucial part.

'Start panting, Babs, don't push!'

Babs clung to Heather's hand, panting for all she was worth. Jackie leaned forward, willing Tom to be gentle with this delicate limb. One twist and it would snap.

He was reaching with his other hand and she saw he now held two legs. She breathed a sigh of relief, even though she knew they weren't out of the woods yet. The baby's buttocks, although tiny, were presenting a problem.

Tom jerked his head round. 'Better do an episiotomy, Jackie,' he whispered.

Jackie was already reaching for the blunt-ended scissors. 'Have I time to inject some lignocaine?' she asked, knowing that a local anaesthetic would ease the pain.

Tom nodded. 'I can hold this stage for a few minutes.'

Jackie injected lignocaine one percent into the patient's perineum, the section of skin between the vagina and the rectum. As soon as she thought this had taken effect, she made an incision to widen the birth canal.

Babs was becoming impatient. 'Can I push?'

'Go ahead,' Tom said, as he manipulated the baby's buttocks out into the birth canal.

Jackie watched as the baby's shoulders appeared, and finally the head. The baby gave a loud howl of protest as it slithered out. She gave a sigh of relief.

'It's a boy,' Tom said, a broad, happy smile on his lips.

His eyes met Jackie's across their patient, and she smiled back, with both relief and admiration at the way Tom had handled this difficult case.

Babs was leaning back against the pillows, looking exhausted but happy. As soon as Tom had cut the cord Jackie handed the baby to his mother.

'Oh, he's gorgeous!'

But suddenly Babs's smiles turned to tears again. 'If only his dad could see him.'

Jackie felt a surge of sympathy. 'Ted may want to come and see him. Why don't you phone him when you're feeling rested?'

Babs clutched the baby to her. 'He won't come back. You see, we agreed not to have kids for a few years till we'd saved up, but I decided I couldn't wait so I stopped taking the Pill. Ted said he couldn't forgive me.'

'All the same, I should give him a call to let him know he's a father,' Tom said gently. 'Now, may I take baby from you for a little while? We need to do a few little tests on him.'

Jackie glanced at her watch as she went out into the surgery car park. She would have to get a move on if she was to be in time for her hair appointment. After she'd arrived back from delivering Babs's little boy she'd had to sort out several administration tasks, as well as checking through and signing the pile of letters which Helen had put on her desk.

Tom had stayed behind at Babs's house with Heather to finish off the baby's tests, suture the episiotomy and make thorough checks on Babs. He hadn't yet returned.

As she climbed into her car she decided she must have been mad to think she could fit in a hair appointment between the end of her surgery duties and going out with Tom—

especially as she wanted to get home in good time for the lighting of the candles on her birthday cake.

As she drove out of the car park she felt a pang of guilt about the fact that she wouldn't be spending her birthday evening with the girls. The first time in sixteen years. Still, they were positively grown up now and very soon she'd have to count herself lucky if they chose to spend time with her on her birthday.

'Only three years younger than I was when they were born,' she said out loud. She found herself hoping they wouldn't make the mistake of getting married early like she had done.

She gripped the steering-wheel as the disloyal thought occurred to her. Had her marriage been a mistake? The mistake had been in marrying too soon, she told herself quickly. That had been the cause of all the problems.

As she manoeuvred her car into a space in the multi-storey car park she pushed away all thoughts of problems in her marriage. Since David's death she'd only allowed herself to remember the good times. Nothing must ever be allowed to spoil his memory. David had been a hero and that was the way she would always remember him.

The hairdressing salon was packed. Jackie realised, as she watched stylists rushing from one client to another and juniors feverishly washing hair while women waited their turn, that she couldn't have picked a worse time.

'How long is it since you were last here?'

Jackie looked in the mirror. Behind her a young man with a long blond pony-tail was attempting to run a comb through her hair. When she'd phoned for an appointment she'd been told that the stylist she'd requested hadn't worked at the salon for ages, but they could recommend Mr Charles.

She smiled. She wasn't going to allow herself to feel intimidated, even though it had taken all her courage to even make the appointment. It was, after all, a drastic course of action she was contemplating! Was it too late to stand up and say she'd changed her mind?

She shifted nervously, smoothing down the capacious green gown that looked as if it would be more at home in the operating theatre.

'It's probably quite some time since I was here. I thought my hair needed cutting. And I'm going out tonight so you could do something a bit different with it?'

Mr Charles smiled at her reflection in the mirror. 'That certainly leaves the field wide open. Perhaps you'd like to look at some of our style brochures so you can chose how you'd like your hair.'

'I really haven't time,' she said quickly. 'Just cut it a bit shorter so that I don't have to wind it up in a chignon to keep it out of the way.'

Jackie saw the smile on the young man's face freeze as he told her it would be a challenge but he would do what he could. Now, if she would just like to go over to the basins, Sharon would shampoo...

After Sharon's ministrations she waited, semi-dried, pretending to flick through a magazine and wondering why on earth she was putting herself through this ordeal. Perhaps Tom would prefer her with long hair, anyway. Perhaps all the effort she was going through to get rid of her tried and tested but infinitely boring chignon would be a waste of time.

'Don't take too much off,' she said, as Mr Charles's reflection appeared once more in the mirror.

'If I might make a suggestion,' the young man said, in the sort of patient voice that adults use for difficult children, 'I'd like to cut it to a length that will fall softly on to your shoulders, but not over them. That way, the natural wave in your hair will lift it and—'

'That sounds good,' Jackie interrupted, glancing once again at her watch. She hadn't time for any more consultation. She would take whatever Mr Charles threw at her now. After all, her hair grew very quickly. She'd soon have it safely back in its chignon if this new style was a disaster.

'Mum, you've had your hair cut!' Fiona said, in amazement.

Jackie hovered by the kitchen door, feeling somehow as if she didn't belong in her own home. Meg was at the sink, filling the kettle. Across the hallway she could see that the dining room table was covered with plates of sandwiches and chocolate biscuits, with the beautiful birthday cake from Marks and Spencer adorning the centre.

'Your hair looks lovely, Jackie!' Meg said, coming across to get a better look. 'It really suits you.'

Jackie smiled as she caught her reflection in the kitchen mirror. Yes, she was pleased with the results.

'You look a lot younger,' Fiona said.

Jackie laughed. 'That's exactly the right thing to say to a woman of thirty-five.'

'Wait till you're forty-seven, like me!' Meg said. 'You'll need more than a new hairstyle to knock the years off. Come and sit down. The birthday tea's all ready.'

Jackie sat down and admired the spread that Meg and the girls had prepared, secretly reminding herself that she mustn't eat too much or she wouldn't be able to cope with a restaurant dinner.

'Lovely sandwiches!' she said. 'Smoked salmon? Where did that come from?'

Fiona smiled. 'We nipped out to the fishmonger's in Estersea at lunchtime.'

'And we had a Coca-Cola at the Smugglers Inn. We thought we might see you there, Mum,' Debbie added, a mischievous grin on her face.

Jackie smiled. 'Well, sorry to disappoint you, but I had a baby to deliver.'

She heard the sound of tyres crunching on the gravel and felt something akin to apprehension.

Meg had already jumped to her feet. 'I'll open the door for Tom. Would somebody like to light the candles on the cake?'

'I hope I'm not too early.'

Jackie smiled at Tom across the length of the table as he came into the dining room.

'No, of course you're not,' Jackie said quickly. 'We're running late because I had a hair appointment and—'

'So I see. It suits you.'

Part of her was thrilled to see the blatant admiration in his eyes, but she couldn't help glancing at her daughters to see how they were taking this. Debbie was busying herself with lighting the thirty-five candles, and Fiona was eating another chocolate biscuit while studying the pattern on her plate as if she'd never seen it before.

'Come and sit down and have some cake, Tom,' Jackie said. 'I may need some help with these candles.'

Tom sat down at the far end of the table. 'I don't think I should eat cake before going out for dinner.'

Debbie put down the matches. 'Oh, you must have a piece, Dr Prestwick.'

Jackie gave her a grateful smile. The ice was definitely breaking!

'We'll give you a small piece, Tom. Stand back, I'm going to attempt to blow out all thirty-five candles in one go so I can get a mention in the *Guinness Book of Records*.'

It took her two attempts before all the candles went out.

'Perhaps next year I'll be successful,' she conceded as she sat down again.

'They don't make cakes that big,' Tom said, with a wry grin. 'When it's my fortieth in December I'm only going to have four candles on it.'

'Are you really nearly forty?' Fiona said, raising her head to look at Tom. 'You don't look it.'

Tom laughed. 'Well, thank you, Fiona. You don't look sixteen. In fact, you look more like eighteen when you're not in your school uniform.'

Jackie watched a slow smile spread over Fiona's face and could see that Tom had said exactly the right thing. It was true that her daughter did look very grown-up in the slim-line skirt and cotton shirt she'd changed into.

She stood up. 'If you'll all excuse me, I'd better go and change.'

'Have another piece of cake, Dr Prestwick,' Debbie said.

'Why don't you call me Tom?'

Jackie felt a certain sense of relief as she ran up the stairs. It seemed as if Tom was making a good impression on the girls. They seemed to be positively enjoying having a man about the place.

She'd better wear something smart. Tom was in a suit so he might be taking her somewhere chic and expensive. Would her wedding and funeral suit be too formal? She pulled out the cream woollen suit that she'd worn on numerous special occasions. It was still in a long plastic bag, straight back from the cleaners.

'Might be a bit warm, but I could take off the jacket in the restaurant,' she told her reflection, suddenly realising how much she liked the new hairstyle.

Yes, it really did make her look younger! Good! She needed a boost to her morale, something to eradicate the mumsy image she'd got used to. She might even have a shopping spree some time soon because there was nothing very exciting in her wardrobe and if she was going to start going out more often...

She teamed up the suit with a green silk shirt and higher-than-usual, hardly-ever-worn, cream strappy sandals.

As she ran back down the stairs she was relieved to hear the sound of laughter.

'So what did you do then, Tom?' Debbie was asking.

'I walked round and round each floor until eventually I found it—'

He broke off and smiled at Jackie. 'I was just telling Debbie about the time I parked in an enormous multi-storey car park, went down in the lift and forgot which floor I was on.'

He stood up and looked across at Debbie and Fiona. 'Do you have lots of homework to do?'

Debbie pulled a wry face. 'I expect we'll be finished in a couple of hours so—' She cut short what she was saying and looked straight at Jackie. 'I hope you have a nice time to-night.'

'Yes, enjoy yourself, Mum,' Fiona said.

Jackie could feel a lump rising in her throat. 'Thanks for my birthday tea. Don't work too hard.'

She followed Tom out to the car. He was holding open her door. She sank down into the passenger seat and waved to the girls. They both waved back as Tom pulled out of the drive.

'I think you've made a hit there,' she said quietly.

'I hope so. My God, I was nervous!'

'You, nervous?' She glanced sideways and saw the expression of relief etched on his finely chiselled features.

'I felt as if I was walking into the lion's den—or I should say, the lionesses' den—when I arrived. You'd made such a song and dance about the girls being unwilling to accept another man in your strictly feminine domain that I—'

'Tom, I'm sorry! I was pleasantly surprised—no, I was delighted—with the way the girls took to you this evening. I wouldn't have believed it before you came along.'

'Well, I'm glad to be accepted but I'll tread carefully.'

'Thanks. As I told you, they've got this big hero-worship for their father and...'

He put his hand across and squeezed hers. 'Don't worry. I won't try to knock their father off his pedestal.'

Why did she have a sudden feeling of apprehension? There was something at the back of her mind that threatened to surface whenever anyone spoke about her gallant husband.

Tom's voice interrupted her thoughts. 'I hope, after the hectic day you've had, you're not going to be too tired to enjoy yourself tonight.'

She smiled as she came back to the present and began to anticipate the evening ahead.

'I feel absolutely fine!'

CHAPTER FIVE

TOM pulled up in front of a small country house, set back from the road. Jackie got out of the car and looked up at the quaint, old, picturesque façade. Ivy climbed the walls and roses rambled around the doorway where a cat was sitting, licking its fur as it enjoyed the evening sunshine.

'It doesn't look at all like a restaurant,' she said. 'More like somebody's home.'

'It's very cosy inside. I came here last week, if you remember,' he said, looking down at her with a wry grin.

She remembered turning down his invitation to go with him.

He put his hand under her elbow to guide her through the open door. A girl in a black dress with a white frilly apron, probably about the same age as the twins, gave them a welcoming smile as she escorted them to a small bar, placing a bowl of pistachios and a plate of olives in front of them.

'Edward will look after you,' she said, as she went away to greet some more people who were arriving.

'Would you like a drink, sir, madam?' Edward, the young barman, put down the cloth with which he was polishing glasses and smiled across the bar at them.

Tom ordered a bottle of champagne.

'We've got to celebrate your birthday,' he said, as the barman uncorked the bottle and settled it in the ice bucket, after pouring out a couple of glasses.

'Happy birthday, Jackie!' He clinked his glass against hers.

'It's been quite a day!' she said, taking a sip of champagne. 'I was so relieved that you were with me this morning when we had to deliver Babs's baby. If I'd been on my own I would have had to talk her into going to hospital. I did a breech birth once but it was in hospital and I had masses of support staff and loads of high-tech equipment.'

'Oh, I think you'd have coped without me.' He topped up her glass.

'Good evening, sir; good evening, madam.'

A tall man with greying hair in a dark suit had come up behind them. 'So sorry I wasn't here when you arrived. I'm Jeremy Mansell, your host. I hope my son and daughter have been taking care of you. Would you like to look at the menu?'

Tom chose lobster for his main course and Jackie said that was what she would like.

'A wise choice,' Mr Mansell said. 'It's fresh today.'

The champagne bucket was carried over to a table by the window when their meal was ready. Tom had elected to go onto sparkling mineral water because he was driving but he said there was no reason why Jackie should stint herself, especially on her birthday.

She tasted her ice-cold melon starter, which had been liberally doused in port. 'Mmm, delicious!'

Together they pulled the lobster apart, sharing the succulent pieces between them. The central plate was soon piled high with discarded pieces of shell.

'It's ages since I had lobster,' Jackie said. 'It's always so expensive. I must admit I wouldn't have dared to order it if you hadn't.'

'My ex-wife always used to order the most expensive item on the menu simply because it was expensive.'

Jackie dipped her fingers in the small finger-bowl beside her plate. She rubbed her fingertips against the piece of lemon that floated in the water as she listened to Tom. This was the first time he'd given her any sort of insight into the character of his ex-wife, and she found she was intrigued by his revelations.

'Charlotte was very ostentatious. Everywhere she went she liked to be conspicuous. She wanted to give the impression that we were an important, wealthy couple. Her father was a consultant and his private practice meant that she'd enjoyed a privileged upbringing—private education, finishing school in Switzerland—'

He broke off. 'Can't think why I'm talking about Charlotte. I—'

'Oh, please, don't stop. I'd like to hear about her.'

The young girl had arrived to clear the plates and bring their dessert. They had both ordered fresh strawberries and cream.

Jackie waited for Tom to continue. He gave her a rueful smile. 'Looking back, I can't think why I married her be-cause we were as different as chalk and cheese.'

'Perhaps she didn't show herself as she really was until after you were married.'

'You could be right,' he said slowly. 'I've never really thought about it. She's an only child and she has a private allowance from her father who absolutely dotes on her. I hadn't realised that basically she was a spoiled brat.'

'Was she difficult to live with?'

He pulled a wry face. 'Absolutely! She used to sulk if she didn't get her own way in everything. She wanted me to spend, spend, spend! She assumed I was wealthy when she first met me and she was hell-bent on spending my money.'

'Why did she think you were wealthy?'

'She knew I'd inherited some money from my grandfather. He ran a successful textile mill in Yorkshire and he left me a nice sum when he died. I've invested it so that it gives me an income besides my salary. I didn't want to simply fritter it away at the rate that Charlotte wanted me to.'

'Did she have a job?'

'You must be joking! She never got out of bed before midday, and that was only if she had to meet someone for lunch.'

'What an amazing lifestyle!' Jackie put one of the strawberries in her mouth. 'These are even better than the ones we had three weeks ago at the strawberry farm.'

He smiled and leaned across the table to take hold of her hand. 'Is it really three weeks since we had our first date?'

'Our first date was supper at your place, five weeks ago.' She looked across the table at Tom, excited by the feel of his hand over hers.

'Tell me some more about Charlotte. What made you split up?'

He withdrew his hand and picked up a spoon. 'I would have thought that was obvious. We were totally incompatible. The final straw for her was when I announced that I wasn't going to go on to become a consultant. Two days later she told me she wanted a divorce.'

'This may be a difficult question but why didn't you want to be a consultant?'

He put down his spoon and leaned back against the back of the upholstered chair. She saw the worried expression in his eyes and heard the intake of his breath before he spoke.

'I was tired of playing God. As a specialist in obstetrics and gynaecology, I was getting too many requests for operations I didn't want to do.' He paused.

'Such as?' she said quietly.

The young girl was clearing their plates. 'Would you like coffee in the drawing room?'

Tom said they would. Putting his starched napkin beside his plate, he stood up. Jackie, impatient to hear more of Tom's revelations, resigned herself to waiting a little longer.

They went into a large, airy room, overlooking a garden full of roses, and out through casement windows that opened onto a covered terrace. Jackie sat down in one of the cane armchairs, covered with multicoloured scatter cushions. A large cafetière of coffee and small china cups had been placed on the table in front of her.

She poured out coffee and took a sip, before looking out across the garden that led down to the estuary. The sun was slowly sinking below the horizon, casting an orange glow over the water.

'On such a lovely evening I know I was right to move out here,' Tom said, his voice husky with emotion. 'I believe I told you it was like taking a step in the dark.'

'Do you sometimes have doubts about it?'

His eyes held an enigmatic expression. 'Doesn't everyone have doubts?'

'What were those requests you had where you felt you were playing God?' she asked, carefully.

He hesitated before speaking, a troubled expression on his face. 'I hated doing terminations.'

He put the palms of his hands together and appeared to be concentrating intensely on what he was saying.

'There were times when the mother's life was threatened if the pregnancy continued, but there were other cases that I felt were in a grey area. I'd gone into the medical profession to save life, not to destroy it. One day, a young woman came to me and asked for her pregnancy to be terminated because she'd just found out she was expecting a girl and her husband wanted a son.'

Jackie drew in her breath but remained silent. She could see that Tom was profoundly moved by the memory of that cathartic occasion.

'Of course I refused, but it made me realise that I didn't want all the trappings of being a consultant.'

He leaned back and ran a hand through his dark hair.

'I wanted to continue working as a doctor, but I wanted to be able to walk away from my work at the end of each day without agonising over whether I'd made the right decisions. Do you know what I mean?'

She nodded. 'I'm beginning to.'

'You remember the lines from the poem, 'What is this life if full of care, We have no time to stand and stare?' Well, it came to me in a flash that I wanted to have more time for the creative aspects of life—my sadly neglected painting for a start. Which leads me nicely on...'

'Yes?'

He was looking at her with that curiously amused grin she'd come to love. What was he up to now?

'I'd like you to come back to look at my paintings.'

Her quick response was automatic. 'I really don't think I should. It's getting late and Meg and the girls will expect me home.'

'I'll call Meg and see how they're getting on.'

'Tom, no!'

He was already punching in the digits on his mobile. He smiled as he listened to Meg's voice. 'She wants to talk to you.'

Jackie took the phone.

'Stay out all night, if you like,' Meg said cheerily. 'I've just tucked myself up in the guest room with a mug of cocoa and the latest Jilly Cooper. The girls are fast asleep.'

Jackie hesitated. 'I won't be late.'

She heard Meg's impatient intake of breath. 'Just enjoy yourself, Jackie. It will do you good.'

As she switched off the phone she reflected that it was easy for Meg to talk like that. She didn't have to wrestle with her conscience.

Darkness fell as they drove back towards Estersea and a crescent moon had appeared in the black velvet, star-studded sky. Tom parked in the drive of his house and opened the door, going ahead to switch on the lights. She followed him into the kitchen and through into his studio in the old wash-house.

'Close your eyes,' he said, when she reached the centre of the room.

She stood quite still, aware only of Tom's breathing inches away from her. He sounded as if he was removing a cloth from one of the paintings.

'Now you can look!'

She opened her eyes and stared ahead at the oil painting in front of her where two swans with their cygnets were swimming on the estuary, their feathers bathed in the colours of the setting sun.

'Oh, you finished it, Tom!' She stood back to see the painting from a different angle. 'It's beautiful!'

'Happy birthday!'

'You mean it's for me?'

Her voice had risen to a squeak in her excitement. 'What a wonderful present! Every time I look at it I'll remember that evening when we watched the swans out there on the estuary and it will remind me—'

She swallowed. It would remind her of Tom. Whatever happened in the future she would always have this memento. On impulse, she held out her hands and reached up to kiss him.

'Thank you,' she said quietly, as she placed her lips on his.

She felt his arms closing around her. As they stood locked together in a movingly sensual embrace she could feel ripples of desire mounting inside her. With one part of her heart she revelled in their closeness, but the rest of her was trying desperately to put the dampers on. As if sensing the struggle that was going on inside her, he pulled away.

'Would you like coffee, or a drink perhaps? You don't have to drive, you know.'

'Coffee would be lovely.'

Coffee would sober her up and bring her back down to earth! For a moment just then she'd thought she was going to lose control of herself and that would have been disastrous.

She took a deep breath to steady her nerves and wandered around the room, looking at Tom's paintings, while he went into the kitchen. There was no doubt about the fact that he had talent. It was so good that he was able to use it at last.

She could hear him filling the kettle. She didn't really want coffee but she wanted to prolong the evening. She could stay all night if she wanted to.

Oh, yes, she wanted to, but she wasn't going to! She wasn't ready for a physical relationship...yet. And when the time came—if the time came—how was she going to handle it? How was she going to square her conscience? Would it get any easier with the passing of time?

He came up behind her and put his hands either side of her waist. 'Come and have some coffee.'

She followed him through the kitchen and into a small sitting room. The squashy cretonne-covered sofa looked inviting. He poured out two mugs from a battered old orange-painted tin jug.

'I bought this jug from a junk shop when I was a student. I had to keep it well hidden from Charlotte when we were married. It didn't go with the image she wanted to portray in our carefully colour-coordinated house.'

Jackie smiled. 'It's good you can joke about it. You don't appear to have any hang-ups about your marriage.'

'I wish I could say the same thing about you,' he said gently. 'How long are you going to go on carrying a torch for David?'

She drew in her breath. 'It's so difficult to banish the memories.'

'You must try,' he whispered.

He moved closer on the sofa, his arms reaching out to

hold her. She hesitated for a fraction of a second, before allowing herself to give in to the sensuous feeling that was sweeping over her.

He nuzzled his mouth against her hair. 'Try to forget the past.'

She moved her head and he kissed her, gently at first and then with a mounting passion that was sweeping her along with him.

His caresses were sending shivers of excitement down her spine. She gave herself up to the sensuous waves of passion mounting inside her. As he pulled her down to lie beside him on the sofa she felt like a flower that had been withering in the desert before the coming of the rains.

'We'd be much more comfortable in bed,' he whispered huskily.

She hesitated, knowing full well that was what she wanted. She told herself that she didn't have to stay the night, but at this moment she wanted, more than anything else in the world, to make love with Tom.

He took her hand and led her up the stairs, pushing open the door to a large, extremely masculine room.

The bookshelves were overflowing so books had been stacked in piles on the floor, and a half-finished picture of a ship was propped against the huge oak wardrobe. The four-poster bed in the centre of the room dominated the room. Dark green drapes were tied back to reveal crisp white cotton sheets.

She sensed that Tom was finding it difficult to control his passionate urgency as he led her over to the bed. He was being oh, so gentle with her as they lay down on the cool cotton sheet, but she recognised that he was holding back, as if wanting to savour each step of their love-making.

He pulled her into his arms again, his kiss tender yet demanding. She sensed the powerful strength of his muscular, athletic body as she moulded herself against him. Waves of passion were sweeping her along. She was reaching the point of no return. Soon he would take her completely. They would consummate their love and...

She stiffened in his arms, even as she clung to him. 'Tom, I can't!'

He loosened the grip of his arms around her and leaned back against the pillow, breathing heavily.

She pulled away from his arms, reaching out to the bedside table for a tissue and dabbing it against her eyes as she tried to come to terms with the floods of guilt that were sweeping over her.

She swung her legs over the side of the bed, feeling suddenly very shy and self-conscious. Whatever had possessed her to come up to Tom's bedroom? She pulled the green silk shirt over her head and made for the bathroom, carrying her clothes in a tangled heap.

When she emerged, fully clothed, Tom was also dressed and sitting in a huge armchair by the window, staring out over the garden.

'Come here,' he said huskily. 'Isn't that a beautiful moon up there?'

He pulled her onto his lap and she rested her head against his shoulder.

'I'm sorry,' she said quietly. 'I shouldn't have led you on. I—'

He put a finger over her mouth. 'Shh...no recriminations. It's been a wonderful evening, just being together.'

She looked out through the window at the moon. Down below in the estuary the water was flowing peacefully out to sea. The feeling of turmoil was passing.

'I'd better take you home now,' he said gently.

Neither of them spoke on the short journey back to her house. Tom carried the painting inside and propped it against a wall in the dining room.

'Goodnight, Tom. Thank you for making my birthday so special. The dinner...and everything...'

They were standing in the hall by the door. He kissed her briefly, his lips barely making contact with hers.

She leaned against the door after he'd gone, listening to the sound of his car driving away down the lane. She wasn't sorry that they'd begun to make love. The sensuous feelings he'd roused in her had been exquisite. But she was glad she'd stopped short of going the whole way. She would have been racked with guilt. She would have—

'Is that you, Jackie?' Meg was coming down the stairs. 'I didn't expect you to come back. Shall I make a cup of tea?'

Jackie sighed as Meg went through into the kitchen. Her friend would want a blow-by-blow account of her evening and she wasn't sure how much she wanted to tell her. She took a couple of mugs from the cupboard and watched Meg as she filled the kettle.

'How were the girls after I left?'

'Fine! Perfect angels, in fact. Fiona did her piano practice. She's talented, isn't she?'

'Yes, she is.'

'Well, come on, tell me what happened. Why didn't you stay out?'

'Meg, I've only known Tom five weeks and—'

'That's not the real reason, is it?'

Jackie leaned back against her chair. 'How well you know me! I'm not ready for a relationship, Meg.'

'But David died five years ago,' Meg said gently. 'Isn't it time you started making a new life for yourself? The girls are nearly grown-up. When they leave home you'll be all on your own and—'

'Meg, because of the gallant way that David died I get awful pangs of guilt about forming a new relationship. I—'

'Jackie, don't you think that David would want you to be happy now?'

She looked across the kitchen table and saw the troubled expression in Meg's eyes. For a few seconds neither of them spoke. It was Jackie who broke the silence.

'I think he would want me to be happy,' she said carefully, 'but I think he would want me to stay faithful to his memory.'

'I think you're mistaken, Jackie. I don't think David would want you to keep faithful for ever, to turn down an opportunity of loving someone else. I think you should go ahead and have a relationship with Tom. I'm sure that's what David would have wanted.'

'Meg, you're a good friend, but you're only saying this to quieten my conscience and—'

'No, Jackie, you're wrong!'

Meg stood up and poured the boiling water into the teapot, standing with her back towards Jackie.

'I've known David longer than you have, you know. We were at medical school together, if you remember. I was the one who gave him a reference when he came to work in your father's practice.'

'Yes, but I'm the one who was married to him, Meg. I think I should know my own husband better than anyone else, shouldn't I?'

'Probably... Mostly... Perhaps.'

Jackie felt confused and puzzled by Meg's attitude. What was she leading up to? She had the distinct impression Meg was hiding something. Meg brought the teapot over to the table and began to pour out.

'I remember once when David and I were in our final year, working on the wards. Now let me remember exactly...'

Meg paused, as if searching for the right words. Jackie remained silent.

'Yes, there was this patient who told us she was going to be faithful to her dead husband for ever and David said—'

'Meg, you're not making this up, are you?'

'Let me finish! David told the patient that nobody should ever spoil their lives by staying faithful to someone who'd died.'

'Are you absolutely sure that's what David said, Meg?'

Meg looked up at the ceiling and gave a sigh of exasperation. 'Of course I'm sure! So, in my opinion, you should stop torturing yourself and get on with your romance. Tom's not going to wait for ever, you know.'

Jackie picked up her mug of tea. If only she could believe her! But why shouldn't she? Meg had never lied to her before.

'It's so good of you to be concerned about me, Meg,' she said quietly. 'Thank you.'

To her surprise, she saw tears in her friend's eyes.

'That's what friends are for,' Meg said gruffly. 'I'm going back to bed. See you in the morning.'

Jackie sat on alone in the kitchen, listening to the steady ticking of the clock on the wall. She would love to take Meg's advice...if she could only be sure her friend was telling the truth.

Maybe she should take a chance, a step in the dark, as Tom had done.

She curled her hands round the warm mug, remembering how she'd clung to him this evening, remembering his caressing hands, the sensuous feel of his lips... It would be impossible to go along with a platonic friendship. That wasn't what Tom wanted—and it was certainly not what she wanted. From now on she was going to listen to her heart not her head!

For the next couple of weeks Tom was politely friendly at the surgery but he didn't make any attempt to see her outside working hours. She threw herself into her work—when she was in the surgery she didn't have time to worry about her personal problems.

Mark Trimble and his mother came to see her during morning surgery. The little five-year-old was as lively as during his last visit and made a beeline for the toys that Jackie kept in the corner of her room. Jackie gave Mrs Trimble a welcoming smile as she sat down, propping her shopping bag against the desk.

'So, is Mark improving since we started the injections?' she asked.

'He's not sneezing as often, Doctor, but once he starts he can't stop.'

Jackie glanced down at the notes that Sister Saunders had made when she'd started the desensitising treatment at the beginning of June.

'Apparently, it's cat fur that's the real culprit, isn't it?'

'Mark loves our little Suky. She sleeps on his bed every night.'

'Well, that's why Mark sneezes most when he wakes up in the morning.' Jackie clasped her hands in front of her as she looked across the desk.

'Mrs Trimble, do you think you could arrange for someone to look after Suky for a couple of weeks while I try another form of treatment?' she asked quietly.

Mark looked up from the toy cars he was arranging on the garage forecourt and scrambled to his feet.

'I want Suky to stay with me,' he said, as he walked over to the desk, staring up at Jackie.

Jackie pulled him onto her lap. 'That's what we all want, Mark. But you'll get better more quickly if Suky goes away for a little while.'

'My mother would have her,' Mrs Trimble said.

'How about that, Mark?' Jackie asked. 'Do you think Suky would like a holiday with your grandma?'

'She might,' the little boy conceded.

'And while Suky is having her holiday, will you pop in every day to see me and I'll try to make you better?'

The little boy looked interested. 'How will you make me better?'

'Well, I'm going to give you a little prick in your arm each morning and—'

'Oh, you mean an injec...an injection,' Mark said. 'I've had lots of those.'

'Well, this one's a very special one,' Jackie said, lifting Mark off her lap as she went over to her drugs cupboard.

She selected a phial, snapped off the top and drew up the required dosage. She'd read about this drug in one of her medical journals a few months ago and had ordered a small quantity. Apparently, it had been developed by a vet for use on humans because he'd come across so many people who couldn't tolerate cat fur. It had passed all its tests and had proved to be a very useful drug.

'It's something of a wonder drug,' she said, as she returned to her desk.

'You mean it's magic?' Mark asked, his eyes wide.

Jackie smiled. 'I hope so. Can you hold up your sleeve for me, Mark?'

The little boy pulled up the edge of his Thomas the Tank Engine shirt and looked the other way while Jackie swabbed his arm, before injecting the fluid.

'What a good boy you are,' she said, putting the empty syringe into a kidney dish.

Mrs Trimble smiled. 'He's getting used to injections.'

'Will you be able to bring him in each morning for a couple of weeks?'

'I'll bring him in on our way to school. Do you think I could come in a bit earlier so that he's not late, Doctor?'

Jackie said she was usually in the surgery by half past eight and would treat Mark as soon as they came in.

'Thank you, Doctor. See you tomorrow. Come on, Mark, leave the toys now.'

'Can I borrow this lorry, Doctor?' Mark asked, holding up a small red vehicle.

Jackie smiled. 'Yes, of course. If you bring it back tomorrow you can borrow a different one.'

'Great! Bye, Doctor,' the little boy said, taking hold of his mother's hand.

Jackie's next patient was a tall, slim, dark-haired woman with a worried expression. On checking the case notes, Jackie found she was Susan Dawson, thirty years old, had two small children and her husband had been killed in a car crash two years before. She'd moved to the area only recently and this was the first time Jackie had seen her.

Jackie smiled at her patient. 'What can I do for you, Mrs Dawson?'

The young woman shifted uneasily on her chair.

'I've come to see if you'll give me a check-up and see if it's OK for me to go on the Pill.'

'Of course. If you'd like to go into the cubicle over there and remove—'

'Do you think I'm doing the right thing, Doctor?' Susan Dawson blurted out. 'I mean, it's only two years since Gordon died and some people might think it's too soon.'

Jackie leaned back in her chair. 'You mean too soon to start another relationship?'

Susan Dawson nodded. 'Mike and I get on so well. I've been holding him off but he's getting so frustrated. I thought we ought to wait a bit longer, but now I find I'm wanting it as well. It's just that I get this awful guilty feeling. You see, I still love Gordon—I always will—but now I want Mike.'

She put her hands on Jackie's desk and stared across at her with pleading eyes. 'So I've decided not to wait any longer. To be honest, I've been in a bit of a rut since Gordon died. It was such a shock. I just didn't want to go out, didn't want to see anybody, didn't want to do anything except look after the kids. And then Mike came along and…well, I suppose you could say he swept me off my feet, Doctor, whatever that means.'

'I'm so happy for you,' Jackie said, smiling. 'It sounds like the best thing that could have happened to you. So let's start by giving you a check-up.'

Jackie's examination revealed that there were no gynaecological abnormalities and she was able to tell Susan Dawson that she was in perfect health.

'So, just enjoy being with Mike,' she said, handing over a packet of Pills.

Susan Dawson smiled happily. 'Thanks, Doctor. You've certainly set my mind at rest. I wish I'd come to see you sooner, instead of worrying on my own about it.'

Jackie watched her patient leave and then sat back in her chair, thinking about how similar her own situation was. Tom had suggested that she was still carrying a torch for David and it was true. And she felt guilty about embarking on a physical relationship with Tom.

She pushed the thoughts to the back of her mind as she continued to see her next patients.

As she closed the door on her last patient, after the long list of the morning, she told herself that she would be lucky if Tom asked her out again after the way she'd behaved.

She went over to the computer and wrote up the notes of the last patient, before switching off and leaning back in her chair.

She'd made such a fool of herself on her birthday evening! Having agreed to go to bed with him, she'd then messed the whole thing up. What an idiot he must have thought her! And why should he ever want to repeat the experience? She'd advised Susan Dawson to enjoy her new relationship and yet she herself couldn't cast off the past. She knew, instinctively, that it was Tom when she heard the light tapping on the door.

He stood in the doorway with his hands on his hips, his expressive eyes scrutinising her. 'Busy?'

'No, I've just finished.'

He advanced across the room, looking as if he had something very important on his mind. His voice was firm and clear when he spoke.

'I wondered if you'd like to go up to London at the weekend. There's an interesting exhibition at the National Gallery. I'm going anyway and I thought you might enjoy it.'

'I would! Yes, that would be lovely!'

'Do you really mean that?'

He seemed surprised by her enthusiasm. 'I mean, you won't have problems escaping from home?'

She smiled. 'Don't worry. I'll get myself a pass-out.'

He came closer and leaned across the desk. 'You look...you look somehow different.'

'Better or worse?'

'Definitely better! Have you had some good news or something?'

'You could say that.'

She kept her tone deliberately light. She didn't want to discuss Meg's comforting theory about David, especially as she wasn't sure it would stand up to being scrutinised. She was simply taking it at face value and enjoying the feeling of freedom it gave her.

And Susan Dawson's happiness was also helpful. If her patient could form a new relationship after two years then surely *she* could bring herself to change after five.

'Well, then, I'll pick you up on Saturday morning about nine. We can drive up and park at my brother's apartment in the Barbican. If you have any problems getting away—'

The intercom was buzzing. 'I can deal with the problems, Tom. Yes, Helen...'

As she listened she could feel apprehension sweeping over her.

'I'll go out there.' She put the phone down. 'Ethel Dunton, a dear old patient of mine, has scalded herself with a kettle full of water. Bill, her son, says she won't let him call the ambulance. She's asking to see me.'

'Would you like me to come with you, Jackie?'

'Yes, I would. Thanks.'

It would be good to have an objective influence. She was so fond of Mrs Dunton that she might find herself becoming too distressed by the situation.

'If only Bill had bought an electric kettle, as I'd suggested!' Jackie said, as Tom drove her up the narrow farm track. 'They have this heavy, archaic contraption, permanently boiling on the hob. It was an accident waiting to happen. I would have bought them a kettle myself but I thought I might offend them.'

The kitchen door was wide open. Bill, a large, stocky, florid-faced, middle-aged man, came to meet them. A confirmed bachelor, he'd cared for his arthritic mother and kept the farm going since the death of his father some twenty years ago. He'd always been there when Jackie had come on visits when she was a child, and she'd been impressed by what a kind, caring, compassionate person he was.

As he approached them she could see the expression of fear in his dark eyes. She put out her hand and grasped his. 'How's your mother?'

'Not good, Doctor.'

'This is Dr Prestwick, Bill.'

'How do you do, sir?'

Jackie hurried inside, the two men following. Ethel was lying on the black leather, horsehair couch beside the fire, moaning softly to herself.

'Mrs Dunton, let me have a look at you. It's me, Jackie.'

'Oh, bless you, love. It's my arm. I was just trying to lift the kettle when—'

'May I have a bowl of cold water, please, Bill?'

When he'd brought it, Jackie carefully held Mrs Dunton's arm, still covered by the sleeve of her dress, in the bowl.

'I'm going to remove your sleeve, Mrs Dunton. It will be easier for you if I cut it. I hope you don't mind.'

Jackie pulled scissors from her bag and cut through the soggy sleeve. Cautiously, she peeled it back, feeling relieved that, although red and swollen, the skin was still intact.

'I'm going to have to take your wedding ring off because your hand is beginning to swell.'

The old lady looked at her finger. 'Never had it off since my wedding day. I'd rather—'

Tom leaned forward. 'If we don't take it off now, Mrs Dunton, we might have to cut it off.'

Jackie gently eased the ring off her patient's already swelling finger. Ethel had lost weight over the years and the ring had recently become too big. But Jackie could see that the swelling from the scald would have soon prevented her from removing the ring if they'd delayed any longer.

'Only just in time,' she breathed as she handed the ring to Bill.

'That cold water feels nice and soothing, dear,' Mrs Dunton said, closing her eyes.

Jackie explained that she was cooling down the arm to reduce the swelling. 'There's some blistering, but fortunately the skin is still intact.'

After a few minutes Jackie lifted her patient's arm out of the water and put it on a splint, securing it with a sterile bandage.

'I won't be able to make my own tea with that thing on,' Mrs Dunton said, with a wry grin.

'Bill's going to buy you an electric kettle, aren't you?' Jackie said, looking up at her friend enquiringly.

Bill nodded sheepishly. 'I've been going to get around to

it for ages. I'll go into Colchester as soon as I can find the time. But I've been so busy that—'

'I'm going into Colchester today,' Tom said quickly. 'I'll buy one and you can pay me when I bring it out tomorrow. We'll need to come and see your mother.'

'Thanks, Tom,' Jackie said, as, having made their farewells, she climbed back into the car. 'I'll leave you to do the house calls tomorrow. I think Mrs Dunton's arm will heal, don't you?'

'Well, the healing process is always difficult to predict with older people, isn't it? Everything takes much longer. We'll just have to wait and see. I'll check on those blisters tomorrow.'

'And let me know how she is when you've seen her. I'm very fond of her. I know it's unprofessional but some patients are just so special, aren't they?'

'Have you known Mrs Dunton a long time?'

She leaned back against the passenger seat. 'As long as I can remember. When my dad brought me out on his house calls I used to toddle around the farmyard, talking to the cats and the hens. Bill would bring me a glass of milk and a biscuit and sit with me outside the kitchen door when it was sunny.'

Tom took one hand off the steering-wheel and placed it over hers. She kept absolutely still, revelling in the feel of his fingers. It was the first physical contact they'd had since that poignant evening two weeks ago. It was magic to feel close to him again.

She was going to make it work between them! No more backward glances.

CHAPTER SIX

As JACKIE looked out of the car window she could see that the strawberry season was nearly over. The signs outside the farms were now advertising raspberries. The summer was slipping by so quickly.

She looked across at Tom as they drove along the country lanes towards the London road, and wondered what the day ahead would bring.

'Tell me something about your brother with the flat in the Barbican—won't he mind you bringing an uninvited guest?'

He glanced sideways, momentarily taking his eyes from the road as he smiled at her. She liked his relaxed appearance today. He looked ready to enjoy himself and she wanted to join in the general mood of being totally off duty.

'Actually, Jonathan won't be there,' he told her. 'He lives part of the time in Paris. He's in computers—quite a high-powered executive, I believe.'

He gave a low laugh. 'Different temperament altogether from me.'

'Who does your brother take after in your family?'

'Difficult to say. He's adopted and we've never met his natural parents. My mum and dad were childless for the first few years of their marriage so they decided to adopt a six-week-old baby. Then, when Jonathan was three months old, hey presto! Mum found she was pregnant with me.'

Jackie smiled. 'That often happens, doesn't it?'

'There's only eleven months between us. My dad's patients, who didn't know that Jonathan was adopted, used to ask if we were non-identical twins.'

'As an only child, I've always envied people who grew

up with someone their own age. That's why I was thrilled
when I had twins. When they were small they always had a
playmate, even though they often used to fight like cat and
dog. Do you get on well with your brother?'

'Yes, we've always been very close to each other. It was
great fun growing up together. I think being so different
helped in a way. Nowadays, we don't see very much of each
other because of our career commitments.'

Tom stopped chatting as he negotiated the speedy slip road
onto the A12. Jackie could see heavy lorries trundling along,
carrying the loads they'd picked up from the ships that
docked at Harwich. They passed a large, people-carrier type
of car which was tightly packed with fidgeting and laughing
children, a harassed-looking dad trying to concentrate on the
driving.

Two small children were strapped into seats facing back-
wards in the back of the car—twins perhaps? she wondered.
They smiled and waved their half-eaten packets of crisps.
Jackie waved back.

The joys of family living! The traumas and tantrums which
sometimes threatened to outweigh the beneficial elements of
this exhausting way of life. It didn't seem possible that
Deborah and Fiona could ever have been so small.

'Nice family in that car,' Tom said, now cruising easily
along in the fast lane.

'You noticed them too? I expect they're going up to
London for a day out. We used to do that. I mean, when the
children were very small we'd take them up to Hyde Park
for a picnic, maybe go to the zoo, visit the Tower. They
loved it, but we were always shattered when we got back.'

She felt Tom's hand stealing over hers. He was thinking
she might be choking up with nostalgia. But she wasn't. At
last she found she could be totally dispassionate about the
family life she'd enjoyed when David was alive. She'd succeeded in consigning it to the past.

A feeling of elation swept over her as she turned again to watch Tom. He looked so handsome in casual clothes. His chinos and open-necked shirt made him appear much younger than his thirty-nine years. Both of his strong, sensitive hands were back on the wheel now as he negotiated the dreaded roadworks. She waited until they were safely out the other side before she spoke again.

'You were telling me about your brother. Is he married?'

He smiled. 'Very much so. Five children—three boys, two girls. They're based in their house in Paris with their mother, Suzanne, and Jonathan commutes at the weekends.'

'Sounds complicated.'

'Oh, it's much easier than it used to be in the old days, you know. The channel tunnel makes life much simpler for Jonathan.'

He paused. 'And he and Suzanne are very happy together. If you love someone very much you can always find a way around the obstacles.'

She swallowed hard. That was so true! She looked out of the window. They were nearing the city now, slowly edging their way through dense traffic. Tom jockeyed for position to get into the correct lane, before turning off at the Barbican into the underground car park.

He stopped outside the porter's window. An elderly, white-haired, bespectacled man leaned out.

'Why, hello, Dr Prestwick. Nice to see you again, sir, after all this time. Where've you been hiding yourself?'

'I'm working out in the wilds of Essex now, Jim.'

The porter grinned. 'Bit quiet for you out there, isn't it? Cows and chickens for company! Although I see you're not alone today.'

Jackie smiled at the porter, who had stepped out of his little cubicle to get a better look at her.

'This is Dr Brent, Jim. My partner.'

'Oh...oh, I see.'

The porter pressed a button and the barrier swung upwards so that Tom could drive in.

'I think he jumped to the wrong conclusion when you told him I was your partner,' Jackie said.

Tom laughed. 'He was meant to. Salt of the earth, old Jim, but as nosy as they come. He's seen everything there is to see but he's still terribly old-fashioned. Calling you my partner gives you a certain status in the morality stakes.'

'We're only parking the car, for heaven's sake!' Jackie said, glancing around the dismal dungeon as she opened the passenger door, climbed out and placed her feet on the cold, inhospitable concrete floor.

He grinned. 'But we'll need to go up to the apartment for a coffee or something. I always have to leave a note for Jonathan to say we've been here.'

They took the lift to the third floor. Tom produced a key and opened one of the identical doors that led from a long landing.

She was pleasantly surprised as she walked into the large airy living room that looked out over well-tended gardens. Tom filled the kettle, humming quietly to himself.

She sank onto a chair overlooking the gardens and allowed Tom to wait on her with coffee and biscuits. As he wrote a note to his brother she went through into the bathroom.

Glancing in the mirror before freshening her lipstick, she decided that the new hairstyle had been a good idea. It had completely changed her appearance.

She smiled. She was no longer the little mouse scampering after her young, spending all her days working and all her evenings and weekends cloistered in the bosom of her family. She was getting her life together at last. And about time, too! The doldrum years were over.

Don't be too complacent, said a little niggly voice inside her head. You've yet to prove you can sustain your elation. There's many a slip between... No! She wouldn't think any further than today. She smoothed her hands over her cream linen trousers, which had become creased in the car. She put the matching jacket back over her crimson silk shirt.

She had to admit that a recent spending spree was partly responsible for her new-found confidence in her appearance. But being with Tom was the most significant factor. Love was a wonderful beauty aid!

Leaving the bathroom, she peeped into the open door in front of her. The master bedroom had an unmistakable female touch stamped upon it. Frilly white drapes at the window complemented the white lace counterpane on the huge bed and the thick white pile of the carpet.

For an instant she wondered if Tom had ever brought anyone else to this apartment and was surprised at the feeling of jealousy that swept over her. She didn't mind hearing about his ex-wife but she couldn't bear the thought that there might have been other women!

The National Gallery was crowded. In some places they had to queue to get a decent view of the pictures, but it was worth it. Jackie was enthralled by what she saw.

Time stood still as she wandered from painting to painting, carefully checking in the catalogue to see that she didn't miss anything.

Occasionally Tom would put his hand under her elbow and guide her across to see a painting he was particularly fond of, but otherwise he left her to form her own opinions.

Emerging from the gallery in mid-afternoon, she realised she was hungry. She hadn't thought about lunch while she'd been inside. A street vendor was selling fruit from a barrow.

'I'd love a peach, Tom.'

He chose the two biggest peaches on the barrow. They carried them across the road into Trafalgar Square and sat by the fountains to eat them. She giggled as the succulent juice ran down her chin.

When she'd finished the peach she rolled up her sleeves and rinsed her hands in the cold water of the pool, carefully avoiding the spray from the fountains splashing nearby.

'Well, that took care of lunch,' Tom said, reaching out for her hand, before saying jokingly, 'Your tiny hand is frozen. I'd better warm it.'

He rubbed both sides with his fingers and she felt a tingle of desire creeping over her.

'Let's walk,' she said quickly.

He held her hand as they wandered through the Saturday crowds down to the Thames and along the Embankment, watching the swirling river as they approached Big Ben.

They crossed the road to stand outside Westminster Abbey, looking up to admire the magnificent façade. The ethereal sound of choirboys singing to the accompaniment of the great organ floated out through the open door.

Tom's fingers gripped hers as he led her along towards St James's Park. They crossed to the middle of the bridge over the water and stood admiring the Canada geese whose feathers were shining in the sunlight.

Jackie looked across the park to see if she could make out the roof of Buckingham Palace. 'Let's go and see if the Queen's in!'

'Maybe she'll invite us in for tea.'

'No, the flag's not flying,' Jackie said, as they emerged from the park. 'What a shame!'

'We could go back to the apartment for tea,' Tom said quickly. 'I'll even cook supper for you as we missed our lunch.'

She hesitated only a fraction of a second but Tom noticed.

'Or, if you prefer, we can have a meal in the West End and go to a show.'

'No, I don't want to be too late home. I'd like to go back to the apartment. It would be nice to relax, kick my shoes off and put my feet up.'

He hailed a cab and they went back to the Barbican. Closing the door of the apartment behind them, Tom told her to make herself at home while he made a start on the supper.

'Need any help?' she called, curling up on the sofa as she listened to him moving about in the kitchen.

He emerged from the kitchen, carrying a bottle of wine and two glasses. 'Everything's under control. I've whipped up the eggs. I hope you like Spanish omelettes. I found peppers, tomatoes and onions so I'm going to chuck the whole lot together and hope for the best.'

'Delicious!'

He handed her a glass of wine. 'And there's a lettuce which is begging to be used up so I'll make a green salad.'

She took a sip of her wine. 'You seem very much at home here.'

'Jonathan and I have always shared everything. I make a point of sending him a case of wine and a Fortnum and Mason hamper occasionally in return for his hospitality here. When he was first starting out in business he used to come and stay at our house in London and now he always says he's glad to be able to repay me.'

He sat down on the sofa and patted the seat beside him. She put her glass down on the little coffee table and snuggled against him. It seemed so natural that she should adopt this position. She felt as if she'd known him all her life.

He leaned down and kissed the top of her head. She smiled as she looked up at him. The expression in his eyes was one of sensual hunger. He needed her as much as she needed him, but could she totally satisfy him? Could she really give one hundred per cent of herself?

He tilted her chin with his finger and smiled. 'Don't worry about it.'

She gave him a rueful smile. 'You can read me like a book, can't you?'

'Certainly can. You're nervous. You think I've brought you here so I can have my wicked way with you.'

His tone was light and bantering, his expression now totally enigmatic.

'Tom, I'm not nervous. I think—' She broke off, searching for words.

'I think I should cook the omelette,' he said wryly.

She followed him into the kitchen, leaning against the cooker as he poured the mixture into a huge omelette pan. Looking at him now, she discerned that he was the nervous one! And it wasn't the cooking that was making him nervous because it was obvious he'd been rustling up omelettes since his student days.

And why shouldn't he be nervous after the way she'd behaved last time? She moved away to sit at the kitchen table and stir the oil and vinegar dressing that Tom had prepared, before turning the green salad in its large wooden bowl.

Should she explain that she'd got herself sorted out—that she was sure that images of the past wouldn't haunt her if they made love again?

Her heart was reaching out to him as she watched him bringing the heavy pan over to the table. With an exaggerated flourish he tipped the omelette onto a central plate.

'*Voila! Madame est servie!*'

'Mmm! Excellent! Delicious! Everything I expected from a five-star restaurant like this!'

He grinned. 'And a five-star cook!'

'Must be your surgical training. They always say surgeons make good cooks.'

'You're absolutely right. Cookery and surgery are very similar. You gather together your ingredients—in the case of surgery you'll need a patient, of course—and then you get some knives, forks and spoons...'

'Mix everything together...' She was laughing now. It was a good feeling, sharing a meal with Tom after a day out together. She could certainly get used to this! In fact, she wanted this to go on for ever...

'Jackie, why are you looking at me like that?'

'Like what?'

'As if you'd never seen me before.'

'Perhaps I've never really seen what you were like—deep down,' she said.

'And what am I like—deep down?'

She put down her fork as she hesitated. 'You're special.'

'Thank you,' he said, his voice husky. 'I think you're pretty special yourself. Would you like coffee?' he added, pushing his empty plate away.

'Later perhaps,' she said carefully.

Their eyes met. She saw the flicker of recognition in his eyes as she stood up. He came round the table towards her.

'Do you really want this?' he asked quietly, his voice showing his concern for her.

She nodded. 'I want us to make love. It seems the most natural thing to do at the end of a perfect day.'

He pulled her gently into his arms, kissing her forehead, her cheeks and then her lips. She sensed the urgency springing up inside him and felt her own answering response.

'Let's go to bed,' he whispered huskily.

In the bedroom, as they undressed each other, she could feel the wild abandoned longing growing deep inside her. Her fingers were all thumbs as she unbuttoned his shirt. He lifted her onto the bed and threw back the sheet, before pulling her into his arms.

A deliriously, heady mood had driven all thoughts of reality from her head as she clung to him. She gave herself up to the waves of passion that were sweeping over her. He was being tender, oh, so tender and gentle with her, and she wanted more. Her fingers moved to caress him so that he would know, without a shadow of a doubt, that she wanted him to take her completely.

As he entered her a moan of delight escaped her lips. This was the fulfilment she needed him to give her. As she experienced the thrusting, virile rhythm deep inside her she felt wave after wave of ecstasy coursing through her body until the final climax transported her away to a state of heavenly unreality...

She must have fallen asleep. As she opened her eyes she saw Tom leaning over her, a loving, tender expression on his face.

'Wake up, sleepyhead. I've brought you a cup of tea.'

'What time is it?'

'Time to leave the smoky old city and go back to the cows and the chickens. Unless you want to stay the night?'

He pulled her into his arms. She smiled up into his eyes. 'I'd love to—but not tonight.'

He kissed her gently on the lips, the kiss of a deliriously happy, satisfied lover. She stirred in his arms and sat up, reaching for the cup of tea he'd placed on the bedside table. Glancing at the clock, she realised that they'd better get a move on.

Loud music was blaring from the house as Tom steered the car into the drive. A couple of motorbikes were parked against the kitchen wall.

Jackie frowned. 'What on earth's going on?'

'Looks like the girls are having a party.'

A tall young man with red hair was emerging though the open kitchen door. He leaned against the wall and began to roll himself a cigarette.

He smiled. 'Hi! I'm Greg. You must be the parents. Debbie said we couldn't smoke inside the house.'

Jackie was glad that Tom was following her as she went into the house. She wasn't sure what she was going to find!

The Chinese carpet had been rolled back in the sitting room and Fiona and Debbie were doing some kind of weird dance in the middle of the floor, while a tall, fair-haired youth lounged on the sofa eating what looked and smelled like a freshly made bacon sandwich.

Fiona smiled 'Hi, Mum.'

Debbie stopped dancing and reached for the volume switch on the CD player.

Fiona frowned. 'Hey, don't turn it down, Deb! I'm enjoying this.'

'It's much too loud,' Jackie said. 'Have you had a good day? Any messages?'

'Yes,' Debbie said. 'Meg popped in after she'd done the morning surgery. She'd brought some sausages so we had a barbecue lunch and spent the afternoon in the garden. She was just leaving this evening when the phone rang—somebody asking her to go and see a patient,' Debbie said.

'But we're subscribing to the replacement doctor service now,' Jackie said. 'They're supposed to be dealing with all our house calls tonight.'

'Well, she had to go,' Fiona said. 'About an hour ago. I thought it would be a good idea to get some friends in to keep us company so I rang Greg.'

'And Greg brought his friend, Wayne,' Debbie said. 'Wayne was hungry.'

Fiona began dancing again. 'Can we turn the music up again, Mum? We're just getting to the bit where—'

'Oh, I nearly forgot!' Debbie interrupted. 'Meg's left you a note. It's here, behind the clock.'

Jackie took the piece of paper. Tom leaned over her shoulder so they could both read it.

Meg had written, 'Helen phoned. The doctor service contacted her to say a patient was insisting on seeing someone from the Benton practice. I'm going to investigate.'

Above the music Jackie heard the phone start ringing. She went to the kitchen to answer it, the decibels seeming to be a fraction lower there.

'Meg! I'm just reading your note.'

'I'm glad you're back. I'm at Lorraine Dewhirst's house. She's thirty-six weeks pregnant and feeling ill. She's your patient, isn't she?'

'Yes. What's the problem?'

Jackie's mind raced back to the last time she'd seen Lorraine a couple of weeks ago. She'd been coming in to the surgery every week since she'd been put on a special diet but she'd missed her appointment last week.

'She's very distressed about her headaches.'

Jackie felt a wave of apprehension sweeping over her. 'Lorraine hasn't complained of headaches before. I've been trying to keep her weight down.'

'Can you come out to see her?'

'Of course. I'm on my way.'

She looked up at Tom as she put the phone down. She didn't know anything about these friends of her daughters and was reluctant to leave them on their own.

'Will you stay and hold the fort while I'm away?'

He smiled understandingly. 'Of course. Sure you wouldn't prefer me to go out to see the patient?'

She hesitated. It was a tempting idea, but she was the one who'd seen Lorraine through the pregnancy so far and she could be so difficult, always insisting on seeing Jackie.

'Thanks, but I'd better go.'

Meg opened the door as soon as Jackie had parked the car.

'Thanks for coming out, Jackie.'

'That was the least I could do for you. Where's the patient?'

'Upstairs. She's on her own because her husband's not coming home from the oil rig for another couple of weeks. Do you want me to stay, or...?'

'No, you've had a long day.'

She ran up the stairs to her patient's bedroom.

'Lorraine, how are you feeling now?'

She looked down at Lorraine's flushed face as she reached for the pulse in her wrist. Immediately she could feel the dangerously rapid pulse rate.

'It's these headaches, Dr Brent. They started last week. That's why I didn't come in to see you—well, if I'm honest, I didn't want you to weigh me. I slipped off the diet a bit...um...a lot! But mainly it was the headaches that kept me at home.'

Jackie pulled out the sphygmomanometer from her medical bag. Her apprehension deepened as she took a blood-pressure reading. Headache and hypertension. Two cardinal signs out of the three which indicated that a patient might be going into eclampsia, the medical condition which could be fatal to both the mother and the baby.

She sat down on the bed and took her patient's hand while she considered the best course of action. The third cardinal sign which indicated pre-eclampsia was protein in the urine. She could check her patient's urine now or she could get her straight into hospital without delay and let the hospital staff take over.

That was the safest course of action. Once Lorraine was in hospital an obstetric team could decide whether or not it was necessary to induce the baby. And they would have the full back-up of all the necessary obstetric equipment.

But she had to get Lorraine in there quickly. It was Saturday night and the ambulance service would be stretched to the limit with drunk drivers, road accident patients and domestic dispute victims.

She came to a decision. Gently she explained to her patient that it was necessary to take her to the hospital.

Lorraine frowned. 'Is it because I've put on so much weight?'

Jackie decided this wasn't the time to say that the extra weight hadn't helped her condition. 'It's the headaches,

Lorraine. And your blood pressure's a bit high. Now, if you can just lean on me, we'll put your dressing-gown on.'

Minutes later Jackie had made her patient as comfortable as she could in the back of the car and they were on their way. She'd made a quick call to the hospital to alert the obstetrics team.

As she pulled up in a parking bay at the front of the hospital, a porter and a nurse came out with a trolley.

'Don't leave me,' Lorraine said, reaching out for Jackie, who took hold of her hand and went with her to the obstetrics unit. An obstetrician, two midwives and a nursing sister met her at the door.

'Hello, I'm Dr Brent.'

'Is this our pre-eclampsia patient?' Sister asked. The team was already surrounding the trolley.

'I haven't done a urine test but that's my provisional diagnosis. Lorraine has a very bad headache and high blood pressure.'

'Thanks for bringing Lorraine straight here, Dr Brent,' the obstetrician said. 'We'll take over now.'

Lorraine looked up at Jackie from the trolley. 'Do you have to go?'

Sister took hold of Lorraine's hand. 'We'll take good care of you now, Lorraine.' She smiled at Jackie. 'Thank you, Doctor.'

She felt a pang of sympathy for Lorraine, being left on her own, but she knew the obstetrics team would take good care of her. She said goodbye to her patient and asked Sister to keep her informed.

As she drove away from the hospital she wondered what she would find at home. It was hardly an ideal situation she'd left Tom in. The combination of the twins, their boyfriends and the loud music was probably driving him mad!

She paused halfway down the lane, wound down the window and listened. Not a sound. And then the silence was shattered by engines spluttering to life. Two leather-clad figures on motorbikes raced towards her, pulling in to the side of the road as they reached her car.

'Thanks for the sandwiches,' Wayne said, bending down towards her window with a cheery grin.

The other boy, she remembered him being called Greg, leaned forward. Her interior light shone on his hair and she saw that the vivid red was actually his natural colour. His eyebrows were a bright ginger colour.

'Your old man thought it was time we went home,' he said, as he leaned his leather-clad elbow on the side of her car. 'Thanks for having us.'

She smiled. She couldn't, in all honesty, say it had been a pleasure. 'Drive carefully!'

She glanced in the mirror as they roared off down the lane and told herself not to be judgemental. They seemed nice enough lads. But so young! No wonder they'd called Tom her old man! Obviously, the girls hadn't explained who he was and they'd jumped to conclusions.

She drove the last few yards home, opened the door and went through into the sitting room. Tom was sitting in a chair by the fireplace. The girls, close by on the sofa, were watching television. He stood up and walked across the room to meet her.

'Come and tell me about the patient,' he said, going through with her into the kitchen. 'What was the diagnosis?'

She sat beside him at the kitchen table as she explained all the medical details of Lorraine's case.

He nodded. 'It's a good thing you've got her into hospital. That's exactly what I would have done with the same diagnosis. Are they going to keep you informed?'

'Sister's going to phone me.' She hesitated. Should she tell Tom the boys had called him her 'old man'? Perhaps not!

'I saw the boys riding off down the lane.'

'Lethal contraptions, those machines! I told them to drive carefully.'

'So did I.'

He stood up and pulled her to her feet as his arms encircled her in a warm embrace.

She found herself wishing he didn't have to go. If only he really was her 'old man'! The thought of snuggling next to his virile, athletic body all night was deliciously tempting. She could feel his male hardness as he held her close. He was wanting to make love again. She was sure he would accept if she invited him to stay.

But how would the girls take it? The practical voice inside her head niggled at her.

'I'd better go.'

He was pulling away from her. Maybe he'd been reading her thoughts again and had decided to make the decision for her.

'See you in the morning.'

He kissed her briefly on the lips and strode briskly over to the door.

After he'd gone she went into the sitting room. Credits were rolling on the TV screen.

'Good, that's the end of the film.' She reached for the remote.

'Did you have a nice day, Mum?' Fiona asked, leaning back against the sofa.

'Yes, thank you. I'm definitely ready for bed. How about you?'

Debbie stood up. 'Come on, Fiona.'

'Are you serious about Tom?' Fiona asked.

Jackie drew in her breath. 'It depends what you mean by serious. He's a good friend. I'm very fond of him.'

'But he's not going to replace Dad, is he?'

She went over and sat down beside her daughter. 'Fiona, nobody's ever going to replace Dad,' she said gently. 'Dad was unique, just as Tom is unique. They both have a place in my life.'

'But do you love Tom as much as you loved Dad?' Fiona persisted. 'Because—'

'Fiona, stop being so personal!' Debbie interrupted. 'I think it's nice for Mum to have a boyfriend. We've got boy-friends.'

'Yes, but we don't go around sleeping with them, do we?'

'Not yet,' Debbie said. 'But when we meet somebody we really like we'll probably want to, won't we, Mum?'

Jackie swallowed. This conversation was getting out of hand. She'd always answered the girls' questions on sex whenever and wherever they arose. Once in the middle of the supermarket, as she'd pushed her trolley passed the fro-zen fish counter, nine-year-old Fiona had asked in a loud voice, 'Does it hurt, Mum?'

She remembered saying absent-mindedly, 'Does what hurt?'

'When the daddy puts the sperm in the mummy, does it hurt?'

She'd tried to ignore the flapping ears of a couple of old ladies nearby as she'd replied, as quietly as possible, 'Well, actually, Fiona, it's rather nice.'

And Fiona had smiled with relief and said, 'Oh, good! Perhaps I'll try it when I grow up.'

Now the girls really were almost grown-up, and their ques-tions didn't get any easier!

'It's best to love somebody before you sleep with them,' she began carefully. 'And you should really be thinking about a long-term relationship—marriage would be the ideal situation. But if you want to talk to me some more when you think you're falling in love, I'll—'

'Of course we'll talk to you about it,' Fiona said. 'I'm glad you explained contraception to us when we first asked you. We had a lesson on it in biology and I told Miss Herbert that Debbie and I knew all about it because our mother was a doctor and she would put us on the Pill if we needed it.'

Jackie drew in her breath, wishing she could have been a fly on the wall in that particular lesson!

Fiona looked at her. 'Well, you would, wouldn't you, Mum?'

'We'd have to have a long chat about it first,' Jackie said carefully. 'I mean, we'd have to discuss who the boyfriend was and—'

'Don't worry. I haven't yet met anybody I'm tempted to lose my virginity to,' Fiona said. 'When I do you'll be the first to know, Mum. I'm glad I can talk to you. You're more like a big sister than a mum now that we're grown-up. That's why we care so much about what happens to you.' She leaned across and kissed her mother on the cheek.

'Goodnight, Mum.'

Simultaneously, Debbie kissed her other cheek. 'Goodnight, Mum. I'm glad you enjoyed your day in London.'

Fiona, leading the way, paused by the door.

'Contraception won't be a problem. It's all the other emotional bits I find difficult—like falling in love. How will I know it's the real thing?'

'Oh, you'll know, all right!'

She saw the startled look that passed between her daughters and wished she'd modified her enthusiastic tone.

There was a long pause that seemed to go on and on before Fiona spoke again.

'I can tell you're speaking from experience, Mum. So, are you going to marry Tom?'

She hesitated. 'I might.'

'Has he asked you?' Debbie said.

'No.'

'Will you tell us when he does?' Fiona said.

Jackie crossed the floor, put both arms around her daughters and hugged them.

'Of course I'll tell you. Because you're part and parcel of the whole set-up. Tom can't marry me without involving you two as well. So I may have to ask your advice.'

'I know what advice I'll give you,' Fiona said firmly.

'Time for bed,' Debbie said, taking her sister's hand and dragging her up the stairs.

Jackie leaned back against the cushions of the sofa, listening to the sounds of the girls in the bathroom. There was a constant, low buzz of conversation.

They were discussing her and Tom. She'd been plunged into a family situation which wasn't going to be easy—either way. If Tom did want to marry her he would be taking on the three of them.

And if he didn't...

She felt a stab of something akin to real physical pain. The idea of life without Tom was becoming unthinkable.

CHAPTER SEVEN

'GOODNESS! You look happy today!' Helen said. 'Monday morning, and you look like the proverbial cat who licked the cream. What's happened? Did you win the lottery?'

Jackie looked across the reception area and smiled. 'I had a nice restful weekend for a change, apart from being called out to Lorraine Dewhirst on Saturday evening. Have we any more news from the hospital? Sister phoned me on Sunday morning to say they'd delivered the baby prematurely because there was a danger Lorraine might go into eclampsia.'

'There's a fax just in which says mother and baby are doing well, and Lorraine is asking if Dr Brent will visit her in hospital.'

'I'll check my schedule—maybe I can find a spare half-hour this afternoon.' Jackie turned towards the stairs.

'Don't dash off, Jackie. I've just made a fresh pot of tea. Come and have a mug of tea with me. Or you can stand on ceremony, insist on your rights as the senior partner of this practice and ask me to bring the best china upstairs to your room, Doctor.'

Jackie sat down in a chair in the reception area and studied the fax from the hospital.

'That's better!' Helen said, smiling as she poured out two mugs of tea and settled herself near Jackie. 'So, how did the weekend really go?'

Jackie took a sip of her tea and continued to study the fax.

The waiting-room door opened and Mrs Trimble walked in, holding Mark's hand.

'Hope we're not too early for Mark's injection, Doctor, only I don't like him being late for school.'

Jackie put down her tea and stood up. 'Of course you're not too early, Mrs Trimble. Come up to my room. It won't take a minute.'

'You haven't time to play with the toys this morning, Mark,' Mrs Trimble said, as Jackie drew up the required dose.

Mark pulled a disappointed face, but rolled up his sleeve and turned his head away.

'Good boy!' Jackie said, as she completed the injection.

'Didn't feel a thing!' Mark said proudly. 'See you tomorrow, Doctor.'

As the door closed Jackie's intercom buzzed.

'Yes, Helen,' she said patiently.

'You haven't finished your tea, Jackie.'

She hesitated. She could say she was too busy but Helen would only seek her out later to carry on where they'd left off. She would have to say something about the weekend.

'I'm on my way, Helen.'

'There must be a good reason for you to look so good at this hour of the morning,' Helen began, as soon as Jackie was settled once more in the reception area. 'A little bird told me you were going out with a handsome doctor who works not a million miles from here.'

Jackie put her mug down beside a pile of case notes and gave Helen a bright smile.

'Oh, you mean the art exhibition we went to? It was fantastic. Well worth a visit if you have the time, Helen. There was a marvellous picture by Monet. You know the one where—'

'Didn't know you were so enthralled by a few old pictures,' Helen interrupted dryly. 'What happened afterwards?'

'We came home and I went out to check on Lorraine Dewhirst.'

Helen smiled. 'I'm not convinced, but I can see you're not going to tell me anything. Well, whatever it was, it's certainly put the colour back in your cheeks and I'm delighted for you.'

She stood up and poured more tea into Jackie's mug. 'I was only thinking the other day that it was about time you stopped playing the grieving widow. You've carried a torch for David far too long. He didn't deserve it, you know. He was no saint.'

Jackie put down her mug and stared at Helen, a feeling of dismay churning inside her.

'Just exactly what are you trying to tell me, Helen?'

Helen's eyes flickered. 'David's always been hailed as a hero so you placed him on a pedestal. But have you ever asked yourself if he deserved such blind adulation?'

'Come to the point, Helen. Everybody knows that David saved Meg's life so, in my book, that constitutes a hero. He lost his own life because of it. The ultimate sacrifice, I would say. Don't you think that was a brave act?'

Her heart was pounding with apprehension. She'd never known anybody to question whether David deserved his place as a hero. Especially not Helen, who'd always been so loyal to him in the past.

Helen put out her hand and touched Jackie's sleeve, as if trying to pacify her. 'Look, all I'm saying is that you need to think about yourself more. David would have done.'

Jackie was even more confused. 'What makes you think David would have behaved any differently to me if he'd been the one who was left behind?'

'Because I've known him longer than you and—' She broke off as the outer door opened and Tom walked in.

Jackie saw the easygoing smile on his lips and her heart went out to him. Being together on Saturday had made them both so happy. It was impossible to hide it. She waited to see if Helen was going to make comments about Tom's care-free expression but, uncharacteristically, nothing was forthcoming.

'Good morning, ladies.' He walked over towards them, picked up the teapot and poured himself a cup of tea.

'There's a fax from the hospital about Lorraine Dewhirst,' Jackie said. 'I told you on the phone they'd induced her and she'd had a baby boy, didn't I? We've got all the details here. I'll go in and see her this afternoon.'

As she started up the stairs Helen followed her.

'Look, Jackie, forget what I said about David. Maybe I spoke out of turn—me and my big mouth!'

'Don't worry. I've forgotten already.'

She went into her room and sat down at the desk, knowing full well that she wouldn't be able to forget. Twice in the past few weeks it had been hinted that she hadn't known David as well as she'd thought, first by Meg and now by Helen. What was she to make of it? Was there some dark secret they were keeping from her?

The door opened and Tom walked in. 'What was all that about?'

He closed the door behind him and crossed over to her desk, leaning over to kiss her on the lips. She savoured the delicious moment but almost immediately afterwards she found herself worrying again about what Helen had said.

'Helen was trying to tell me something about David but then she changed her mind and said she was speaking out of turn. She seemed to imply that I didn't know what David was really like, that he wasn't the saint we've all tried to make him out to be.'

She heard the sharp intake of Tom's breath. 'I would say she's trying to give you some very good advice.'

She frowned. 'Meg hinted at the same thing. Do you think they both know something that I don't?'

He hesitated. 'It's possible. Would it make any difference if you knew?'

'I think it would help me to put the past behind me if I thought I'd really been carrying a torch for too long.'

'But I thought you'd finally put the past behind you on Saturday when we made love,' he said quickly.

He moved swiftly round the desk and put his arm around her shoulder, pulling her against him.

'Making love with you was wonderful,' she began, as she tried to sort out her confused emotions. 'But being able to sustain a loving relationship without any thought of the past...isn't going to be easy.'

'I see.' He was walking towards the door.

'No, you don't see, Tom! You don't understand.'

'I think I understand perfectly.'

'Tom!'

He closed the door. She listened to the sound of his feet echoing away down the corridor. She longed to run after him but she could hear one of his patients already walking past her door.

The intercom buzzed; her first patient was waiting. She would have to make it up with Tom at the end of the morning, if she could. Babs White, carrying her baby, opened the door and came in.

'Well, isn't he lovely?' Jackie said, trying to forget her problems as she got up from her desk to take hold of Babs's little boy. 'I don't have to ask how old you are because you were born on my birthday.'

Babs smiled. 'Seems like yesterday. Doesn't the time fly?'

'It certainly does!' Jackie remembered the breech delivery she and Tom had performed at Babs's house. 'What are you calling him?'

'We're going to call him Paul.' Babs paused and smiled. 'My boyfriend, Ted, has come back home again.'

Jackie felt a surge of vicarious happiness for her patient. 'Oh, I'm so glad! I hoped he would.'

'I phoned him after Paul was born but he didn't come back until this week, and now he's really happy we've got a baby—says he should never have left me on my own. He was worried about how we would manage, but now he's got himself a better-paid job so it looks as if we're going to be OK. And we've decided to get married.'

Jackie smiled. 'That's great news! So, Ted is the reason you've come for your postnatal check-up early, is he?'

Babs gave a shy grin. 'We couldn't wait until you'd given me the all-clear. I hope I haven't done any damage—internally, I mean.'

'Was there any pain or discomfort when you had intercourse?' Jackie asked, remembering the sutures in Babs's perineum.

Babs shook her head. 'No, we were very careful and it felt...well, I enjoyed it.'

'Let's take a look, shall we? I'll put baby Paul in the cot here while you hop up onto the couch.'

Jackie settled the baby in the cot, washed her hands and put on sterile gloves. She shone her angle-poise lamp carefully along Babs's perineal area. The stitches had healed well and there were no further lacerations. Gently, she checked her patient internally.

'Everything's back in place, Babs. You're in excellent shape. I'll take a look at Paul while you're getting dressed.'

Baby Paul objected vociferously to having his ears and nose examined, but became calm and quiet again when Jackie walked him round the room, patting his back and talking to him in a soothing voice.

'He's got a good pair of lungs, Babs! In fact, he's a very strong little boy.'

'Takes after his dad.' Babs hesitated. 'Dr Brent, do you think I could go in and see Dr Prestwick? I'd like to thank him for delivering baby Paul. I didn't realise what a complicated birth it had been until Sister Stanton told me about it afterwards.'

'Of course you can see Dr Prestwick. I'm sure he'll be delighted to see baby Paul.'

Jackie picked up the internal phone and contacted Tom. As she punched in the digits she knew she was glad of the excuse!

'I've got Babs White here with baby Paul, our breech delivery. She'd like to come in and see you when you've got a spare minute.'

'Send her along now. I'll ask Helen to hold the next patient. And, Jackie...'

'Yes?' She waited, her heart pounding as she heard the husky tone of his voice.

'I'm sorry.'

Relief flooded through her. 'So am I.'

'See you later.'

As she put down the phone she could feel the colour rising in her cheeks.

'Dr Prestwick says he can see you now, Babs.'

She got up and opened the door so that Babs could carry the baby out into the corridor.

'Thanks, Dr Brent.'

She watched Babs walking along to Tom's room. It would have been so easy to escort her, but she wasn't sure how she was going to handle their little contretemps. The trouble was she had the feeling that their first quarrel could be magnified into a full-scale difference of opinion if she wasn't careful. They would have to get together and talk as soon as possible before things were blown out of all proportion.

Her list of patients carried her way past the normal lunchtime so that, by the time she could escape, Tom had already gone out to do an emergency house call. Meg was making herself a cup of tea in the deserted reception area. Just the person she needed to talk to!

'Would you like to come home and have a sandwich with me, Meg?' No time like the present for clearing the air!

'That would be lovely, but I haven't time for lunch today. I've got an appointment with my dentist in half an hour.'

'Well, come for tea, then. I'd like...I'd like a chat with you.'

Meg looked surprised. 'Anything in particular on your mind?'

Jackie hesitated. 'It's about David. Helen's been making vague, derogatory insinuations about him and I hoped you could enlighten me.'

She heard the sharp intake of Meg's breath. 'If Helen's stirring things up then she should be the one to explain. But, on second thoughts, perhaps... Look, I'll come down for tea and we'll talk. Can't stop now—must dash.'

Throughout the afternoon Jackie found her thoughts constantly turning to what Meg might be going to reveal. She found it hard to believe that both Helen and Meg had been shielding her from some undesirable secret about David. All the time she'd idolised him, had there been some flaw in his character that made a mockery of her unquestioning adulation?

Perhaps he'd made a pass at one of them—or both. She couldn't imagine it of David, but these things did sometimes happen between colleagues, working closely together. Was that so very awful? That would depend on how seriously...

She told herself to stop speculating. She would know soon enough.

As she walked down the obstetrics ward to Lorraine Dewhirst's cubicle she was still trying desperately to stop wondering about the secret she'd convinced herself that Meg would reveal about David. Meg would enlighten her in a couple of hours' time so she would just have to be patient. Lorraine was delighted to see her. She was sitting up in bed, breast-feeding her new baby, and looked the picture of health.

'Thanks ever so much, Doctor, for all you did on Saturday night. One of the midwives told me that I was lucky you brought me in when you did, otherwise my baby might have died.'

Jackie smiled as a feeling of relief flooded through her. Remembering Saturday night, she was so glad that Lorraine had been delivered in time.

'Has your husband seen him yet?'

'No, they've sent a message to the oil rig and he's trying to get a helicopter to bring him over today.'

After visiting Lorraine, Jackie went along to the gynae-cology unit to see another of her patients who'd had a hys-terectomy. Joanne Walker, a mother of six children who'd been suffering from prolonged and heavy periods, had de-cided to take Jackie's advice and have her womb removed.

Jackie had pointed out that not only would it take away the drudgery of her debilitating menstrual cycle but it would also free her from the worry of having any more children.

To her dismay, she found that Joanne was depressed and weepy. Holding her hand and encouraging her patient to talk, she tried to find out what was worrying her.

'I know I didn't want any more children, Dr Brent, but now that I can't have any I'm wondering if Jack will fancy me any more.' She hesitated. 'You know what I mean—when we're in bed together.'

Jackie knew exactly what Joanne was getting at because she'd had to deal with the same problem several times with other patients.

'Listen, Joanne,' she said gently. 'You and Jack will prob-ably have a much better sex life than you've ever had before because all the worries have been taken care of. And Jack won't find you any different inside. We've simply removed the cradle and left the playpen.'

Joanne's tears turned to laughter. She reached for a tissue and blew her nose vigorously. 'Well, that's a relief! Thanks for coming in, Doctor. You've really cheered me up. I've been lying here worrying and now you've set my mind at rest. I couldn't talk to the nurses in here because I don't know them as well as I know you. Sometimes you just need somebody to talk to, don't you?'

Jackie smiled. 'You do, indeed, Joanne. I'm exactly the same.'

Driving home, Jackie was feeling apprehensive about talking with Meg, but she was hoping that her friend would be able to set her mind at rest.

'Sometimes you just need someone to talk to,' her patient had said to her.

She hoped that, in choosing Meg, she would get the answers she wanted.

Meg was already in the kitchen when she arrived.

'The girls let me in. They're upstairs in their bedrooms, doing their homework.'

Jackie smiled. 'You must have waved your magic wand over them. They usually spend ages over their tea.'

'I gave them both a sandwich to take upstairs, and asked them not to come down for a while because you and I need to talk.'

Jackie's apprehension deepened as she listened to Meg's uncharacteristically serious tone.

'Meg, what I want to know, first of all, is whether you were telling me the truth when you gave me that story about David not believing people should be faithful to a deceased partner. To be honest, it sounded as if you might be making it up. At the time I found it comforting, but I was clutching at straws and...'

She stopped in mid-sentence as she heard the unmistakable sound of a car pulling into the drive. Meg went to the kitchen window.

'It's Tom.'

Jackie drew in her breath. 'That's unfortunate timing.'

'No, it's not. I asked him to come.' Meg was already on her way to the front door.

'So, what's going on?' Tom looked at Jackie as he sat down at the table.

Meg poured out three cups of strong tea, before leaning back in her chair and studying the ceiling. Nobody spoke for a few seconds.

Meg broke the awkward silence. 'Jackie has just asked me if I made up a story I told her about David not believing that surviving partners should remain faithful. Yes, I did make it up. It was a complete fabrication.'

Jackie drew in her breath. 'I suspected as much. But, at the time, I wanted to believe it. It gave me a breathing space.'

Tom cleared his throat. 'Meg, why did you invent that story?'

Meg hesitated. 'I was thinking on my feet at the time. You'd put me on the spot, Jackie, with all your talk about how noble and high-minded David had been. I invented that story.'

She gave a self-deprecating, low laugh.

'It wasn't a very plausible story, I have to admit, but it was the best I could think of at the time.'

'And it worked,' Tom said evenly. 'Jackie was starting to get her life together again. But you haven't answered my question. Why did you invent the story?'

Meg sighed. 'I'd like to be able to say that I was being totally altruistic, that I wanted Jackie to enjoy life to the full, that I wanted her to fall in love with you, Tom, as I had fallen in love with—' She broke off, and Jackie watched, alarmed, as her friend covered her face with her hands. And in a blinding flash she knew the awful truth.

'You fell in love with David, didn't you, Meg?'

Jackie's voice was barely audible but Meg heard.

'It was guilt that made me invent the story. For five years I'd watched you crucifying yourself in your belief that you'd lost the perfect husband, when all the time...' She choked.

'So, were you having an affair with David?' Tom asked, his tone ominously low and controlled.

Meg nodded. 'It started when we were medical students and we met on and off over the years. After I'd been working for your father for a while, Jackie, David asked me to give him a reference so that he could join me here.'

A feeling of emotional numbness was stealing over Jackie. She felt she couldn't take any more awful revelations but she knew she had to keep delving into the past until she found out the whole truth.

'Meg, if you were in love with each other, why didn't you and David marry?' she asked in a whisper.

'David wanted to have children. I didn't. I enjoy being with children who belong to other people. I can hand them back and keep my own independence.'

Tom reached across the table and took hold of Jackie's hand. She could feel the comfort and strength flowing into her. She saw the angry expression in his eyes as he turned towards Meg.

'So I suppose you told him to marry someone else, someone who would agree to have children. And did you promise to be his mistress after he was married?'

Meg nodded. 'I'm not proud of what I did. At the time I didn't know how fond I was going to become of Jackie and the children.'

Jackie's sadness deepened as she remembered how she'd always thought of Meg as the perfect surrogate aunt. The children adored her. How much of the time and care she'd lavished on them had been motivated by guilt?

'Tell me about the night David died,' Jackie said quietly. 'Was it really how you described?'

Meg closed her eyes and remained silent for a few seconds, as if visualising the fateful evening.

'David and I had arranged to meet after evening surgery and...and spend some time together. That was why he came to my room. He didn't know that awful drug addict was threatening me with a knife. I could hear David's footsteps coming nearer along the corridor. The youth heard him too. He pushed the blade of the knife against my throat and dragged me behind the door. If I'd screamed, he would have slit my throat.'

'What happened when David opened the door?' Tom asked quietly.

Meg closed her eyes again and took a deep breath.

'The door opened, David came in and the youth sprang on him, plunging the knife into his back. That was when I escaped—when the two of them were lying on the floor. I knew there was nothing I could do against someone with a knife. I managed to lock myself into Helen's office at the side of the reception area and phone for the police and the ambulance service.'

'Did the man come after you?'

'No. I felt sure he would be waiting outside the door with his knife. I didn't dare open it. I didn't come out until the police arrived and found the man had gone.'

Jackie turned agonised eyes towards Meg. 'And David?'

Meg stifled a sob. 'I stayed with him until the ambulance came, and then I phoned you.'

'And I went to see him at the hospital,' Jackie said, as if in a dream. 'He was having difficulty speaking. His speech was totally incoherent but I knew he was trying to tell me something important, something...' Her voice choked as she thought of David's deception.

Tom stood up and came round the table to put his arms around Jackie.

And, as if mesmerised, Jackie's eyes were drawn to the kitchen door. Tom had closed it when he came in but now it was most definitely open and standing on the threshold, their faces ashen with horror, were the twins. Oh, God, how long had they been standing there? How much had they heard?

Jackie leapt to her feet, but Meg got there first.

'Fiona! Debbie!' Meg was attempting to soothe the sobbing girls.

'Don't touch me, Meg! Get away from me! I never want to see you again,' Fiona said.

Tom walked across to Fiona and put both hands on her shoulders. Jackie watched in amazement as Fiona suddenly buried her head in Tom's jacket. She herself put an arm around Debbie's shaking shoulders.

Tom turned to Meg. 'I think it would be best if you went home, Meg,' he said, his controlled voice barely concealing his fury.

Jackie heard the strong even tone but she knew Tom well enough to recognise the anger he felt at Meg's revelations. She looked across at her friend and colleague and felt nothing but pity. In time she would feel anger too, but all she experienced at the moment was a feeling of deep sadness that her best friend should have betrayed her like this.

She opened the front door and Meg went out. Jackie watched her climb into her car and drive away without looking back.

Returning to the kitchen, she discovered that the girls had stopped crying. Tom was sitting beside them at the table talking in a soothing voice.

'So, you see, nobody is perfect. We all have flaws in our characters and—'

'But I thought Dad was perfect—and Meg, too. And now I've lost both of them,' Fiona said.

She looked up at the wall, at the picture of David, with Debbie and herself sitting on his lap when they were small.

'He was my hero. I idolised him, and all the time he was going behind Mum's back and having an affair with her best friend. How could he do that? I still love him because he was my father but...'

'Fiona, he was only human,' Tom said quietly. 'And humans aren't perfect. Yes, it was wrong of him to deceive your mum. But he's still a hero. If he hadn't gone to Meg's room she might have been the one who was killed.'

'Yes, but Meg had always made out that he was so brave in defending her against this man when all he actually did was walk into the room,' Fiona persisted.

'I'm sure he would have tried to defend Meg if he hadn't been caught by surprise,' Debbie said quietly.

She took hold of Fiona's hand. 'You know what Dad was like. He was a very brave man. Remember that time we were walking through that field and that stallion started to chase us? Dad pushed us both over the wall before he went over himself. It was snorting and stamping its feet at the other side. Whatever he's done, he's still my hero.'

'I suppose you're right,' Fiona said slowly, 'but it's going to take me a while to accept what really happened.'

'Me, too,' Jackie said.

'Oh, Mum!' Both girls reached forward and put their arms around Jackie.

As Tom's arm came around all of them she leaned against him, thankful for the strength he gave her.

'I want you to rest now, Jackie,' he told her firmly. 'I'll take care of Debbie and Fiona. Go upstairs and leave this to me.'

Never had she thought she'd feel grateful to hand over the reins.

As she sank down on to her bed she could hear Tom's deep voice answering the girls' questions, explaining everything they wanted to know.

She closed her eyes and lay back against the pillows. The deep, soothing voice in the room below was lulling her off to sleep.

*   *   *

Later—much later, it seemed—she awoke to find Tom standing beside the bed, looking down at her, his eyes full of tenderness. She started to sit up but Tom advised her to keep on resting.

'You've had an awful shock, Jackie. It's going to take some time before the wounds heal.'

He sat down on the side of the bed and took hold of her hand. 'Can I get you anything? Some supper, perhaps?'

She shook her head. 'No, thank you. What are the girls doing?'

'They've gone to bed. They were emotionally exhausted. I think they're already asleep.'

'How do you think this will affect them?'

'Like you, they're going to need time to recover.'

He bent and kissed her on the lips. She reached out and put her arms around him.

She was grieving inside for the sham her marriage had been and she wanted to blot out the memories. She felt as if she couldn't take any more of the sort of emotion that drained away her energy. But at the same time, deep down inside her, she began to feel the wonderful, exciting emotions that being near Tom evoked. These were the sort of emotions that exhilarated her and gave her strength.

She still felt utterly shell-shocked but she knew that if she made love with Tom she could begin to forget the past and start to look ahead to her new life. She sensed that Tom was holding back, trying to resist the physical urges that being close to her evoked.

'Let's make love,' she whispered. 'I need you so much.'

With an audible sigh he pulled her against him, caressing her body with his strong, soothing, sensitive hands. She abandoned herself to his caresses and felt the rising tide of her passion match his, striving for the ultimate orgasmic sensations. His caresses became more urgent. She clung to him, moulding her body against his and revelling in the feeling of him deep inside her, as wave after ecstatic wave flooded through her.

Some time later, curled inside his arms, she smiled up at him. 'You've got a wonderful bedside manner, Doctor. Will you stay with me tonight?'

She saw his hesitation. He ran a hand through his thick, dark hair.

'I think we should give the girls more time,' he said quietly. 'And I don't think I should leap straight into their lives after what they've just heard.'

'You're probably right.'

'The next few weeks are going to be crucial,' he said, his expressive eyes thoughtful. 'It's not going to be easy—for any of us.'

CHAPTER EIGHT

NEXT morning, as Jackie flicked through the post on her desk, her eyes came to rest on one from the regional health authority. Apparently, the new purpose-built medical centre at Estersea was now so successful in terms of patient care that they would like her to consider moving her practice there. She leaned back against her chair. These planning people certainly chose their moments!

Last night her world had been rocked by Meg's devastating revelations and now this! Did they really want her to seriously consider breaking up the practice that her grandfather had founded, the surgery where her father had spent all his working life?

She picked up the internal phone and called Tom.

'Can you spare me a few minutes, Tom? I need your advice.'

He was with her in seconds. 'What's the problem? You sound worried.'

She tossed the official-looking paper across the desk and watched anxiously as he scanned it quickly.

'I simply can't give up everything my family has worked for, can I, Tom?'

He looked up from the letter, an enigmatic expression in his brown eyes.

'I don't think you should dismiss it out of hand,' he said carefully. 'It would certainly mean a more efficient system for the patients. I've been highly impressed with the medical facilities and equipment available to me when I've been operating there each week.'

'Well, yes, I've been impressed myself whenever I've

been down there with a patient,' she conceded. 'But using the facilities occasionally and radically dismantling the entire practice are two completely different ideas. Surely you can see that, Tom? I mean, whose side are you on?'

He came round the desk, putting his hands on her shoulders as she took hold of the letter again.

'I'm not taking sides, Jackie. It's the march of progress. I remember telling you that the same thing happened to my family's practice. My mother told me the patients were delighted with the new purpose-built medical building. And, after all, that's why we're working, isn't it? For the sake of the patients. You've got to give the idea some consideration.'

'Oh, I'll give it some consideration,' she said quickly, 'but I hate the thought of this building being made redundant. It's been in the family for—'

'I know, I know,' he said in a soothing voice. 'My mother went through the same disturbing changes. But in the end...'

'You're actually in favour of moving to Estersea, aren't you?' she said quietly.

He hesitated, seemingly searching for the right words to express his feelings.

'As senior partner, it will be your final decision but maybe it could be for the best. A change of surroundings might be a help in the present circumstances.'

She knew what he was getting at. This building held too many memories, good and bad.

'You could have a point,' she said. 'I must admit I had mixed feelings when I walked in here this morning. I had to force myself not to think about...about what Meg told us last night.'

'Has anyone seen her this morning?'

Jackie shook her head. 'I'm dreading it. All the time I've been going through the post I've been expecting her to—'

She broke off, her eyes coming to rest on a hand-delivered envelope. She would know Meg's handwriting anywhere—large loops and bold flourishes. She tore the envelope open. It was a letter of resignation, short and to the point, saying that Meg felt, under the circumstances, she could no longer work at the surgery. She wasn't going to return.

She looked up at Tom. 'Meg's gone.'

She heard the swift intake of his breath.

'I thought she would. I'm glad,' he said evenly.

'But we'll have to get a replacement as soon as possible.'

'We can get a locum initially, and take our time in making a permanent appointment. Would you like me to call the agency, Jackie?'

'Yes, please. I'll ask Helen to phone round and reschedule the patients—unless you think we can handle this morning's list by ourselves.'

He gave her a long, slow smile. 'I don't see why not. I'm feeling pretty fit this morning. How about you?'

She smiled back, revelling in the electric charge of remembered passion that flashed between them. The revelation of the affair between David and Meg had created a deep-seated ache in her heart, but her love for Tom was like a healing balm, gently soothing her wounds.

'I had a good night's sleep after you'd gone.'

'And how were the girls this morning?'

Her brow creased. 'Subdued. I tried to draw them out but they didn't want to talk.'

'Give them time. They're going to need all the help we can give them. They—' There was a knock on the door and Helen walked in.

'Meg just phoned from Stansted airport. She was just about to board a plane for Greece and wanted to say goodbye to me. What on earth's going on? She said you would explain.'

Jackie looked at Tom, pleading with her eyes for him to take over. She didn't trust her own voice not to break down.

Carefully he began outlining what Meg had told them, but halfway through the disturbing account, Helen interrupted him.

'It's OK. I've always felt it was something like that. I knew what was going on between Meg and David.'

'You knew and you didn't tell me?' Jackie said evenly.

Helen looked defiant. 'Would you have wanted me to?'

Jackie drew in her breath. 'Probably not. At least I had good memories about David for a long time.'

'You kept your memories far too long,' Helen said sharply, before she glanced knowingly at Tom. 'Now it's time to let go of the past.'

'So everybody keeps telling me,' Jackie said. 'Talking of which…'

She handed the merger letter to Helen. 'What do you think about this?'

Helen glanced at it. 'I've seen it coming. I'd say it was inevitable.'

'Not necessarily,' Jackie said quickly.

'How would you feel about it, Helen?' Tom asked.

'Me? I'd take it like a shot. A nice new building like that! This place needs so much spending on it, doesn't it?'

Jackie looked at Tom as Helen left them. 'I wish I could be as objective as Helen.'

He leaned across the desk and kissed her gently. 'You can't change overnight. I wouldn't want you to. But give the merger idea some thought.'

In between patients she found her mind constantly flitting to the new idea. Tom was right. It would be good for the patients. But could she really walk away from all this?

Towards the end of the morning she was in the middle of a chest examination when she heard a squeal of brakes, followed by the sound of crashing metal outside on the main road.

Her patient, Pamela Aldridge, stared up at her from the examination couch.

'What was that, Doctor?'

Jackie fixed her stethoscope back around her neck and went over to the window. 'It sounded like…'

Outside in the road she could see a motorbike and a car meshed together. She opened the door into the corridor to see Tom sprinting past.

'I'll go, Jackie.'

'I'll be with you in a minute. I've almost finished here.'

She turned back to her patient, briefly explaining her findings and reassuring her that her chest was clear.

'Let yourself out when you're dressed, Mrs Aldridge. There's an emergency out there in the road so, if you'll excuse me…'

Tom was leaning over the figure of the young motorcyclist. With a shock of recognition, she saw the leather jacket, leather trousers and distinctive red hair.

'Hello, Greg,' she said gently.

The young man stared up her. 'You're Fiona's mum, aren't you?'

'That's right,' Jackie said.

'There was this cat ran out in front of me. I swerved to avoid it. I think the road had a wet patch. That's why I skidded. Are they OK in the car?'

Jackie could see a woman examining the dent in the side of her car. She looked visibly shaken but not physically injured.

'Yes. I think you're the only casualty.'

'My leg's hurting like hell.'

'I'll give you something for the pain,' Jackie said, taking a syringe from her medical bag. Carefully, she eased off Greg's jacket so she could inject a strong dose of pethidine.

Tom, she noticed, had cut through the leather trousers to

deal with the injured leg. It would have been impossible to remove them intact and avoid further damage to the leg.

'We've got a compound fracture of the tibia and fibula,' Tom said in an undertone to Jackie.

'What have I got, Doctor?' Greg said.

'I'm afraid both bones in your lower left leg have broken, Greg,' Tom said. 'We'll have to get you into hospital so the doctors there can put the leg in plaster.'

'How can you tell it's broken without an X-ray?' the young man asked. 'Is it all wobbly?'

Tom hesitated. Jackie could see the bones sticking out through the skin, making diagnosis obvious, but she didn't expect that Tom would tell Greg. Lying flat on the blanket Jackie had brought out from the surgery, he couldn't see what was going on.

'I would say it's definitely broken, Greg,' Tom said gently. He looked up at Jackie. 'I'll get a stretcher and we'll take him inside till the ambulance arrives.'

Jackie remained in the road, talking quietly to Greg. A small crowd had gathered. Two of the men from the village had taken over the job of controlling the traffic, allowing only one line of cars to pass through.

'Good thing you knew how to give injections,' Greg said to Jackie. 'I'm feeling a bit woozy now, but it's better than all that pain.'

'I'm a doctor, Greg. Didn't Fiona tell you?'

'No, she didn't. I don't know her all that well. We met at a school disco and I gave her my phone number. I was really pleased when she phoned me and asked me out to your place. Will you ask her to come and see me when I'm in hospital, Mrs...er...Doctor.'

'Of course.'

Tom had returned with a stretcher. Alf, the man who worked part time in the surgery garden, was accompanying him.

'Alf's going to give me a hand.' Tom knelt down and carefully fixed the injured limb onto a splint, before easing Greg on to the stretcher.

As Tom and Alf carried Greg inside, the crowd began to disperse. Jackie went over to speak to the woman who was now sitting in her dented car, having moved it to the side of the road.

'Are you feeling all right?'

'I'll be OK. I wasn't hurt. Bit of a shock, that's all.'

'Would you like to come inside the surgery for a cup of tea?'

'That would be nice, but I don't want to miss the police when they arrive.'

'Don't worry, they'll come inside. It will be more comfortable for you in there when you and the young man are exchanging addresses and insurance details.'

'Is he badly injured?' the woman said, getting out of the car.

'His leg is broken, I'm afraid.'

'Could have been worse. He swerved to avoid a cat that ran in front of him. The road was wet so he slithered along and the bike went over on top of him. He didn't stand a chance, poor boy.'

Jackie didn't comment on this piece of information. It was for the police to make out a report of what had really happened. She could hear sirens in the distance. The ambulance and the police were arriving. Greg would soon be taken to hospital where he would get the best treatment for his leg.

'So, is Greg badly hurt?' Fiona stared across the kitchen table at Jackie.

'The bones in his lower leg are broken,' Jackie said gently. 'They've put the leg in plaster of Paris and he'll have to stay in hospital for a while.'

She felt sorry for her daughter as she saw the look of

sadness on Fiona's face. This was the second consecutive teatime when her daughter was on the receiving end of some bad news.

'So he won't be at the disco on Saturday, Mum?'

'Oh, Fiona, don't ask stupid questions!' Debbie said. 'How could he possibly go to a disco with his leg in plaster?'

Jackie flashed Debbie a warning look, which clearly indicated that she was to be kind to her sister.

'People do walk around in plaster, but not usually so soon after an accident,' Jackie said. 'Greg may need traction in hospital.'

'What's traction?' Fiona asked.

'It's a treatment given when the bones of the legs need to be extended or held in place so that the fractured parts will knit together and heal.'

'Will you run me to the hospital this evening so that I can see Greg?'

'Of course I will.'

Jackie felt dead on her feet after her long tiring day in the surgery, but she could keep going for a while longer if she had to. She still had to consider Debbie.

'Will you be OK on your own, Debbie, or would you like to come with us?'

'I want to finish my biology homework.' Debbie paused. 'Mum, do you think…? Could you ring Tom and see if he'll come over? This house creaks when you're the only one in it and it's quiet. It's dead spooky.'

Jackie smiled. 'I'll see if he's in.'

As she picked up the phone she felt a wave of pure happiness sweeping over her. Tom answered on the second ring. He seemed as thrilled as she was that he'd actually been requested to stay with Debbie.

'Tom will be here in a few minutes,' Jackie said, as she put down the phone.

'Great! Do you think he'll help me with my biology? We're doing the skeletal system,' Debbie said.

Jackie laughed. 'So you had an ulterior motive, after all, did you? You'll have to ask him. You can borrow the plastic bones in my old medical student box, if you like.'

'Ooh, thanks, Mum!'

As she walked along the corridor to the orthopaedic ward with Fiona, Jackie suddenly shivered as the memories flooded back. She'd walked along to this very ward five years ago, not knowing whether she would find David still alive.

For some reason they'd put him in the orthopaedic ward. The curtains had been round his bed, she remembered, and the Sister had met her at the door.

These very doors! As she pushed them open she had a sudden flash of memory. She looked down the ward, half expecting to see the blue and white curtains around his bed.

'Are you all right, Mum?'

Fiona had taken hold of her hand. She realised she'd been standing still in the entrance to the ward.

'Dr Brent, so glad you could come.'

Sister was walking towards her down the ward. 'Young Greg's been asking about you. Apparently, Fiona is a friend of his, I believe. Let me take you to see him.'

The curtains were now green, Jackie noticed as she followed Sister down the ward. They'd changed in the last five years. She paused beside the bed where David had been. The curtains were drawn back and a cheery young man was sitting up in bed, headphones on as he hummed to the music, oblivious to what was going on in the ward.

Then, in a blinding flash, she remembered, as if it had been yesterday. Straining to hear David's incoherent words, the only words she'd been able to make out had been, 'I'm sorry.' He'd kept on repeating it amidst the jumble of inaudible phrases.

At the time she'd thought he'd been talking about the row they'd had just before he'd gone out to do the evening surgery. But she hadn't wanted to even think about it. She'd tried to soothe him.

She remembered now that their rows had grown worse over the years, but in the shock of David's death she'd blanked all that out. She'd fixed a rosy glow over the memories of their family life and ignored the occasional twinge of memory that had threatened to undermine it.

What had that final row been all about? She remembered now. David had announced at teatime that he would be away the following weekend, playing golf. This was the third golfing weekend in three months and she'd flipped. She'd pointed out that he'd promised to take the girls swimming. He'd said he would make it up to them, which meant that he'd bring them back some expensive presents.

What a fool she'd been! Golfing weekends, my eye! He'd never even touched his golf clubs from one of those monthly expeditions to the next!

She remembered sitting by his bedside, leaning over him as she'd tried to unscramble the incoherent sentences. He must have been afraid that the whole sordid story would come out and he'd wanted her to hear it from him first.

But the story hadn't come out because the youth with the knife had never been caught and he wasn't likely to go around telling what had happened. And Meg, the only other person who'd been in the surgery that night, had concocted a story that she'd stuck to—until yesterday.

She wondered, fleetingly, if this version was the truth or if there was another one that might be even more damning to the pair of them. It didn't matter any more. It was all in the past.

'Your daughter's with her friend, Dr Brent.'

Sister's voice cut through her thoughts.

'Oh, thank you, Sister. I'll...I'll join them in a moment.'

'Are you sure you're all right? You look a bit—'

'I'm fine! A bit tired. We're one doctor short at the practice.'

'Come and have some coffee. The youngsters won't mind.'

Jackie smiled. Suddenly a large weight seemed to have been taken away from her.

'Thanks, I'd like that,' Jackie said, following Sister into her office.

'How is young Greg?' she asked as she accepted the mug of coffee.

'We've cleaned up the wound and put the whole leg in plaster. We had to put a pin through the heel and fix him in traction so he'll be here for a few weeks.'

They chatted for a few minutes about mutual patients in the hospital before Jackie went back into the ward. She found Fiona and Greg laughing happily together, sharing the bunch of grapes that Fiona had brought with her.

'Do you know how long I'm going to be tied up to this contraption?' Greg asked Jackie.

'Probably a few weeks, I'm afraid. When both the bones are broken it takes a while to get them properly aligned, and then they have to heal before you can put any weight on them.'

Greg pulled a face. 'Will you come and see me again, Fiona?'

Fiona agreed to come in whenever she could.

Jackie turned her car into the drive and stopped by the front door.

'Thanks, Mum,' Fiona said, her hand on the passenger door. 'Greg said you were marvellous with him when he crashed. And Tom as well. He's a good doctor, isn't he?'

'First class.'

'You like him a lot, don't you, Mum?'

'Yes.'

'Are you going to marry him?'

'He hasn't asked me,' she said quietly.

'Oh, Mum, don't be so old-fashioned! Do you want to marry him, because if you do…?'

The door was opening, letting out a shaft of welcome light. Tom was standing in the doorway. Jackie's heart gave a little hop, skip and a jump. Yes, oh, yes, she wanted to marry him—to spend the rest of her life with him!

She reached for the handle of the car door but Tom was already there, opening it for her. As she stepped out he took hold of her hand and kissed her gently on the cheek.

'How was young Greg?'

Fiona was already in the house, calling out for Debbie.

Tom's arm went around Jackie's waist as he escorted her inside. She explained the orthopaedic details that Sister had given her.

'Let's hope Greg's bones heal quickly,' Tom said. 'Those motorbike crashes can be the very devil. I wouldn't let a son of mine ride a motorbike. They're absolutely lethal.'

'Are you planning to have a son, then?' she asked, feeling decidedly brazen as she looked up at him. Fiona's jibe about being old-fashioned had rankled. Maybe she should make it more obvious how she felt about Tom.

He smiled down at her. 'I'd love to have a son—wouldn't you?'

She hesitated. Was this a proposal? Should she put her cards on the table?

'Mum, come and see the skeleton we've made!' Debbie dashed into the kitchen. 'Come on! Tom helped, but I did most of it myself, didn't I, Tom?'

Tom smiled. 'You certainly did. Come and have a look, Jackie.'

The plastic bones had been strung together in Debbie's

bedroom, hanging from the ceiling. Jackie gave the requisite admiring remarks.

'I'd better be getting back home,' Tom said. 'I'm working on a painting and I'd like to do a couple of hours on it.'

Jackie glanced at him, but his bland expression gave nothing away. She hoped all this domesticity wasn't putting him off. He'd spent the whole evening helping Debbie and now he seemed anxious to leave. Just when she had her own designs on him!

At the door he kissed her gently on the lips. She swallowed the remains of her pride.

'Do you have to go, Tom?'

He looked surprised. 'I didn't want to shock the girls by staying on until breakfast.'

She smiled. 'Who said anything about breakfast? We haven't had supper yet.'

He laughed as he gathered her into his arms. 'You certainly have changed, Jackie.' He kissed her slowly, sensually. 'What are you suggesting?'

'I'm suggesting we start treating the girls differently. I don't think they'll bat an eyelid if you're here at breakfast. In fact, I think they'll be pleased.'

'What makes you so sure?'

'I've finally realised that Debbie and Fiona are virtually adults and we've all got to start leading our own lives.'

The expression in his eyes was tender as he looked down at her, his hand caressing her cheek.

'So would you like to stay for supper and breakfast, or would you prefer to finish your painting tonight?'

He held her close against him, his lips against her cheek.

'Mum, I'm starving,' Fiona called from the sitting room. 'What's for supper?'

'I think it's your turn to cook, Fiona,' Jackie said. 'Come on, Tom. I'm going to open a bottle of champagne. Ethel Dunton's son, Bill, gave it to me when I went out to see how her scalded arm was healing. I thought I'd save it for when I had something to celebrate.'

'So what are we celebrating?' Tom asked, following her into the kitchen.

She opened the fridge and handed the bottle to Tom. 'You can do the honours.'

Then, very carefully, she selected two cut-glass, hardly-ever-used champagne glasses from the back of the cupboard.

'We're celebrating life,' she said slowly, holding out her glass towards him.

The cork popped, and Jackie laughed as Tom scrambled to pour out the champagne before it could flow on to the floor.

'To us!' he said, raising his glass to clink it against hers.

'Are we invited to the party?' Debbie said, coming into the kitchen.

'After you've helped Fiona with the supper. There's some cold ham in the fridge and—'

'Mum, leave it to us.' Fiona had joined her sister and was reaching into the glasses cupboard. She produced a couple of tumblers and held them out with a wide grin. 'Just a teeny-weeny taste, please.'

'Well, as you're not driving, I'll give you a small sip,' Tom said.

'How about you, Tom?' Debbie said. 'Aren't you driving tonight?'

He smiled. 'Your mother's persuaded me to stay.'

Jackie glanced at Fiona and saw her approving grin. Her daughter wouldn't call her old-fashioned again!

'That's good,' Debbie said. 'After supper, would you like to help me dismantle the skeleton?'

'No, he wouldn't!' Jackie said, taking hold of Tom's elbow and steering him out of the kitchen. 'We're going to drink our champagne in the sitting room.'

'I hope they're not going to get a taste for alcohol,' Jackie said, as she settled down on the sofa in front of the fireplace.

The elaborate arrangement of summer flowers that Fiona had fixed in the centre of the fireplace was looking a bit past its sell-by date, she noticed. She would see if Fiona would like to do another one soon.

'I've never allowed the girls to drink before,' she told Tom.

'Don't worry,' he said, sinking on the sofa beside her. 'The latest medical opinion holds that it's best to introduce young people to alcohol in small amounts in their home environment. That way, they're supervised and monitored and parents can explain the dangers of alcohol. Anyway, half an inch of champagne isn't going to turn them into alcoholics.'

She snuggled against him and took another sip of champagne. It was so good to have someone else to lean on— another person to share the responsibilities of being a parent.

She looked up at Tom's handsome profile. The light from the table lamp was casting shadows over his face. He looked more desirable than she'd ever known him to be.

Several minutes passed, during which he held her against him, stroking her hair as they chatted together. Suddenly she realised she wasn't hungry. She wanted to stay curled against Tom for the rest of the evening. In fact, she would have liked to skip supper and go straight to bed!

'Supper's ready!'

Tom pulled her to her feet and, still holding hands, they went into the kitchen together.

There were candles on the kitchen table and a small bowl of flowers. In the centre of the table was Jackie's huge blue and white casserole. Fiona was leaning over it, her hand in an oven glove.

'Sit down, everybody,' she said, as she whipped off the lid. *'Voila!'*

'My favourite!' Jackie exclaimed. It was a dish she'd taught the girls how to make when they were very small.

'What is it?' Tom asked.

'Ham wrapped round celery hearts,' Fiona said proudly.

'With a cheese sauce which I made,' Debbie said. 'The sauce is a bit lumpy, I'm afraid, so you'll have to imagine that's extra cheese.'

Jackie sat at her dressing-table, brushing her hair. They'd finally cleared away the supper things and the girls had gone to bed. No comments had been made about the fact that Tom was staying the night.

Had the girls really accepted him as one of the family? And, if so, how did Tom feel about this? Was he happy to play surrogate parent? Would he have preferred to go back to his bachelor house and spend the evening painting?

It had been a riotous meal in the kitchen, full of laughter and fun, but was that what Tom wanted? Was she rushing him into…?

She saw his reflection in the mirror as he came back into the bedroom from the bathroom. His eyes were full of tenderness as he approached her.

She turned and he took her into his arms, his hands caressing the skin beneath her robe. Deftly he undid the knot at her waist. The robe slid to the floor and he pulled her against him.

She gave a low moan of anticipation as he picked her up and carried her over to the bed.

Their love-making was tender, gentle, unhurried, and afterwards they lay entwined in each other's arms as they slept.

Awaking in the morning to find Tom beside her was almost too perfect. Jackie looked down at his slumbering body and made a wish that nothing would change their new-found happiness.

They had everything now that they had each other. Nothing could prevent them from staying together for ever...could it?

Why did she always have to find a tiny doubt at the back of her mind?

CHAPTER NINE

'WELL, when can we expect to hear wedding bells, Jackie?'

Jackie stopped halfway up the stairs. She'd been trying to sneak in while Helen was in the treatment room chatting with Rosemary Saunders.

It had been a particularly hectic morning at home, the girls having announced that they'd been invited to spend the day with a friend who lived in Frinton.

'It's OK, Mum, we're invited for breakfast,' Fiona had announced last night as they'd all been sitting round the supper table. 'You won't have to worry what we're up to for the whole day.'

'I suppose you'll need me to transport you over there?' Jackie had said.

'Well, it's a bit cross country, isn't it? Too far to walk and the buses around here are practically non-existent,' Debbie had said apologetically. 'So, if you wouldn't mind getting up a bit earlier, Mum...'

Jackie turned to look at Helen. 'I don't know about wedding bells! I'm simply looking forward to the day when the girls are old enough to drive themselves around. I've just got back from taking them over to Frinton and the traffic was dreadful. Everybody queueing up to drive through the railway gates and—'

'That's a pity because old Mrs Dunton's son, Bill, phoned to ask if you'd go and see his mum this morning. You must have passed the end of the lane that goes up to the Dunton farm on your way to Frinton.'

'Now she tells me!'

'Come and have a coffee before you go, and tell me how you and Tom are.'

The door from the car park was opening.

'Not now, Helen!'

Jackie started back up the stairs, knowing it would be Tom. She'd rather say good morning in the privacy of her room.

She waited. He didn't appear. She flicked through the post, dealing with the letters that needed automatic replies and leaving the ones which required thought until later. She felt her pulse quicken as she heard his footsteps outside in the corridor.

She smiled, pushing the letters to one side and looking up from her desk as he came in. It was only hours since she'd lain in his arms but she felt the familiar stirring of sensual desire deep inside her. How long could this idyllic state last?

He was smiling his tender, confident smile—the smile of a man who knew he was loved. Could that be the reason why he hadn't mentioned anything about making their relationship permanent? Was he content to keep the present arrangement going for a long time? Idyllic as it was, they needed to decide what the future held for them.

She stood up. He came towards her, put his arms around her and kissed her gently on the lips, before sitting down in a chair at the other side of the desk.

'The agency's sent us another new locum,' he said.

Jackie groaned. 'Not another new one! What happened to the one we had last week? I spent ages showing him the ropes.'

'Apparently, he's got himself a permanent job at the new medical centre in Estersea.'

'I see,' she said quietly.

She remained silent as the problem of the merger reasserted itself with a vengeance.

He reached across the desk and took hold of her hand.

'Look, Jackie, don't worry about the new locum. I've just been showing him around Meg's room and he seemed to catch on quickly enough.'

'Yes, but how will he treat my patients? And if he goes out on house calls what's his bedside manner going to be like?'

Tom grinned. 'Probably not as good as mine.'

For the life of her she couldn't think why she was blushing! Tom had a way of making her feel like a star-struck teenager. Still, there was probably nothing wrong in that! Very good for the morale!

'Thinking about the room our locum is settling into, it's strange how we still call it Meg's room,' she said quickly. 'I wonder how she's getting on in Greece.'

'Helen had a postcard from her,' he said. 'Didn't she tell you?'

'No, she's probably trying to spare my feelings. But she needn't have worried. I went through an angry phase but I don't bear her any ill feelings any more. When you fall in love it's difficult to think straight so—'

She broke off in mid-sentence.

He smiled, and she hurried on. 'So, what's Meg up to?'

'The doctor on her favourite Greek island has taken her on and she seems to be enjoying it. I must admit, I can't help thinking it's more than she deserves.'

'No, don't say that, Tom. She was very good to the girls as a surrogate aunt.'

He shrugged. 'If you say so. Now, about our new locum. He said he'd like to see the boss and I told him she was always in a bad mood on a Monday morning.'

'You didn't!'

'No, of course I didn't. I wanted to have the boss to myself for a few minutes because I've got a proposal to put to her.'

She felt a rapid increase in her pulse rate as he leaned across the desk.

'Tell me, Dr Brent, as head of this practice, can you tell me if I qualify for a week's holiday round about the fifteenth of August?'

Her spirits sank. She pretended to busy herself with the calendar as she tried to formulate a reply.

'You'll have been here three months on the fifteenth of August so, theoretically, you could take a week off. But, Tom, think of the staffing situation! I haven't had any replies to the advertisement you placed for Meg's job.'

'That's because I haven't placed the ad yet,' he said quietly.

For a few seconds she was speechless, then she burst out, 'But we decided on the format and—'

'Jackie, I'm convinced that it would be better if the Benton practice merged with Estersea. I've hinted that it's the best course of action several times but...'

'I know you have!' she interrupted heatedly. 'You've been trying to talk me into it, but I want to make up my own mind. I don't want you to railroad me into something I might regret.'

His eyes flickered. 'I only want what's best for you, Jackie. You won't regret it.'

'That's for me to decide.'

He hesitated. 'If you stay on here I won't be staying with you.'

She stared across the desk at him. How could he do this to her? Force her to choose.

'I think you'd better take that holiday,' she said quietly.

'Only if you'll come with me.'

She could feel her spirits lifting again. But the idea was impossible!

'Tom, we can't both leave the surgery for a week!'

'I think we can. Haven't you noticed how the number of patients has diminished since the new medical centre opened? A couple of locums would be ample to keep this place going while we're away. Helen will boss them around and make sure everything runs like clockwork. And when we get back you'll have made your decision.'

She remained silent, realising that she *had* noticed the departure of some of their patients but she'd refused to admit it to herself. She'd told herself the trend wouldn't continue. The patients would prefer the old-style health care they'd had at the Benton surgery.

'When we get back?' she repeated, still in a daze at how quickly Tom was moving on. 'Back from where?'

He took both her hands in his. 'I want to take you to France, to my brother's holiday home near Bordeaux.'

'But what about the girls?'

'The girls are invited. Jonathan and Suzanne are looking forward to meeting all of you. The twins will love being with such a large family. Three boys and two girls. The eldest, Michael, is seventeen; Edward's fifteen, George is thirteen, Felicity and Annabel are four and five.'

She took her hands away from his as she tried to think clearly. The idea of a holiday with Tom sounded too fantastic to be true! She went over to the window and looked out across the garden to the fields and beyond to the tall fir trees on the boundary of her own garden.

If she went right away from here for a while she would be able to put things into perspective. It would be easier to decide about merging with Estersea if she wasn't surrounded by memories. And it would be wonderful to spend a whole week with Tom!

She turned round.

'OK. You'd better make arrangements for an extra locum before the fifteenth because we'll have to show him the ropes.'

He smiled. 'I made a provisional booking with the agency this morning as soon as I'd taken the early phone call from Jonathan.'

'You were pretty sure of yourself! What if I'd refused?'

'Then I'd have had to persuade you.'

He crossed over to the window and pulled her into his arms. He smiled down at her. 'Come to think of it, I would have enjoyed the persuasion.'

His kissed her, gently at first and then more urgently. She responded, feeling the sensuous waves stirring deep down inside her.

There was a knocking on the door. Tom released her from his arms and crossed the room to open it.

'Come in,' he said to the young, fair-haired man on the threshold.

'I hope I'm not disturbing you.'

Tom glanced at Jackie who was running both hands over her rumpled hair, and smiled.

'Not at all. Jackie Brent, this is James Spencer, our new locum.'

Jackie held out her hand. 'How do you do, Dr Spencer? Have you found everything you need in...' she had to check herself '...your room?'

The young man smiled. 'Yes, thank you. Apart from a sphygmomanometer.'

'The one in that room's gone missing,' Jackie said, wondering, as she had done when the loss was first brought to her attention, if the sphyg. was now on a Greek island!

If it was it was entirely by accident, she was sure. Meg must have packed in a hurry and carried her medical bag complete with all the contents. Meg was no thief, simply someone trying to escape quickly from an impossible situation.

'You can borrow mine,' she said, handing the sphygmomanometer over the desk. 'I'm just going out to visit a patient and I don't need to check her blood pressure.'

As she drove out to see Ethel Dunton she couldn't stop thinking about the week she was to spend in France, and the decision she was to make when she got back. Would she like working in a new purpose-built building after all the years she'd been associated with the dear old Benton surgery?

Tom had made it quite plain he was in favour of the merger, even saying he wouldn't remain at the Benton surgery if she insisted on staying put. Did he mean he would take a job at Estersea or was he planning to leave the district altogether? And, if he did, what would that do to their relationship? Would they drift apart?

She had a whole week with Tom all to herself. She would make the most of every minute, just in case their idyllic affair was coming to an end. The idea was too awful to contemplate, but she had to face up to that possibility.

Ethel was delighted to see her. Bill came in from the fields to put on the electric kettle that Tom had bought for them.

'I can manage it myself but Bill won't let me,' Mrs Dunton said, from her armchair by the fire.

The temperature outside was in the seventies but the Dunton fire hadn't been allowed to go out. One of the cats sauntered in and sat by the fender, waiting for Jackie to stroke him as she'd stroked all the previous feline generations at the farm.

Jackie examined Mrs Dunton's arm. The blisters had healed but there was some scar tissue.

'Does your arm give you any pain?' she asked.

'It's no worse than the pain in my hands,' Ethel Dunton replied, holding up her arthritic fingers. 'But the tablets help a bit.'

'I'll give you some more,' Jackie said, delving into her medical bag.

'Thanks, dear. You always were a good girl,' Mrs Dunton said absently.

Jackie reached for her cup of tea. The cat jumped up onto her lap, purring loudly as she stroked him.

'I'll be away for a week from the fifteenth of this month, Mrs Dunton,' Jackie said. 'There'll be a couple of locum doctors, if you need anything.'

'What about Dr Prestwick? He could come out, couldn't he? I like him.'

'Well, actually, we're both away at the same time.'

For a moment Ethel Dunton looked confused, and then she smiled.

'Oh, I see, it's like that, is it? Well, you couldn't be going away with a nicer man. What are the girls going to do?'

'They're coming with us.'

Ethel's smile broadened. 'That serious, is it? Well, congratulations! I hope you'll both be—'

'Mrs Dunton, nothing is settled. It would be a big step if we...if we got together permanently. And there are so many problems... You wouldn't believe how—'

'You take it one step at a time, dear, and it'll all sort itself out. Don't look any further than today and you won't go far wrong.'

Jackie smiled. 'I hope you're right.'

Because that was exactly what she'd decided to do.

On the fifteenth of August they flew to Bordeaux. The girls were wildly excited. They'd only flown a couple of times before but they both agreed it was their favourite mode of transport. After less than two hours in the air they were standing in the arrivals hall at Bordeaux airport, waiting for Tom's brother to arrive.

'There he is!' Tom said.

Jackie watched the tall, fair-haired man as he approached to give Tom a bear hug. It was very apparent that there was an emotional warmth between them. Jonathan might be an adopted brother but Jackie could see that there was a bond as strong as any blood-bond.

The introductions were made and the luggage stowed away in the boot of a massive Land Rover.

'You need a car like this when you have five children,' Jonathan said, as he drove away from the airport.

They were dashing along a motorway, three lanes of fast-flowing traffic seemingly competing with each other as if they were on a race track.

'It's fun being on the wrong side of the road,' Fiona said. 'Did it take you long to get used to it, Jonathan?'

'No, it's very easy really. I'm teaching my son, Michael, to drive now. He's never driven himself in England so it seems natural to him.'

They left the motorway and pulled into the grounds of a small château. A long, straight, tree-lined drive led up to the imposing façade, which was topped by a crenellated roof.

'Oh, it's beautiful!' Debbie said.

'Is this where we're really going to stay?' Fiona asked, in an awestruck voice. 'Do you own this place, Jonathan?'

Jonathan laughed. 'We only own half of it. There's a French couple who live in the other half. It's a bit dilapidated inside so I was able to buy it at a bargain price, and we're gradually doing it up. Are either of you girls any good with a paintbrush?'

'I am!' Fiona said enthusiastically, as she climbed out of the car.

A tall, slim woman, looking incredibly young to be the mother of five children, was coming down the front steps, followed by the four younger children and two Alsatians. She gave a welcoming smile as she held out her hands towards them, introducing herself as Suzanne.

For the whole of the week Jackie found herself enchanted by the place. Jonathan and Suzanne did everything they could to make them feel welcome, and all the children got on well together. She could see that both Fiona and Debbie seemed to be smitten by the handsome, seventeen-year-old Michael, whereas he didn't seem able to decide which one of the twins he preferred.

She watched them going around in a happy threesome, laughing and joking as they slapped paint on the walls of the huge entrance hall or splashed each other in the small swimming pool below the steps in front of the château.

Annabel and Felicity, the two youngest members of Jonathan's family, often played in the shallow end of the pool under the watchful eyes of Edward and George, their older brothers.

Jackie's offer of help with a paintbrush was firmly rejected. Jonathan insisted that she and Tom were to take a holiday. The painting work was intended to keep the youngsters out of mischief if they were getting bored.

So she found she spent a lot of time simply lazing on the sun lounger, closing her eyes and trying to think of nothing but the next delicious meal that would be served up in the shabbily ornate, panelled dining room.

Occasionally she would allow herself to think about the large, airy bedroom, with the balcony overlooking the swimming pool. Through her sunglasses she could see the red drapes, pulled back from the window. She could imagine the wide oak bed, with its ornate, silk drapes, and the cool cotton sheets where she and Tom made love every night, far into the night—and sometimes in the afternoons, too, if they could escape unnoticed!

It was as if she was suspended in time. Decisions could wait! Mrs Dunton had advised her not to think any further than the day she was living. And that was exactly what she was doing.

'I hope I'm not disturbing you.'

Jackie raised herself on the sun lounger to look up at

Jonathan. Tom, only inches away from her, patted the seat beside him.

'Come and sit here, Jonathan. As it's our last day we were making the most of the sun. I don't know what the weather will be like when we get back to England tomorrow.'

Jonathan laughed. 'It's raining. I just checked the world-wide weather report.'

Jackie groaned. 'All good things come to an end. I daren't think about the problems that will be waiting when we get back. Decisions, decisions!'

'Talking of which, have you told Jackie about the job?' Jonathan said, looking intently at his brother.

'What job?' Jackie asked, as a flurry of apprehension threatened to disrupt her peaceful mood.

Tom cleared his throat. 'Jonathan has asked me to consider applying for a post in his company's medical centre. They're expanding so they need more medical staff.'

'You mean Jonathan's company in Paris?' she asked, as a feeling of abject bleakness swept over her.

She could feel that the worst possible scenario was about to unfold. Jonathan was planning his escape from the Benton practice.

'Yes.' Tom said. 'Jonathan's company is based in Paris. It's a unique opportunity.'

She swallowed. 'And?'

'And I've applied,' he said quietly.

CHAPTER TEN

'I WAS going to tell you when you'd made your decision about the Benton-Estersea merger,' Tom said evenly.

They were lying in the large bed, Tom firmly to one side and Jackie to the other, a wide space between them.

Earlier, during supper, she'd tried to appear as if she was enjoying their final evening in the château, but it had been difficult to enter into the spirit of things. She'd been relieved that the youngsters were having such a whale of a time and making so much noise that hopefully nobody noticed the strained atmosphere surrounding Tom and herself.

But now, when they were alone at last, all she could think about was the fact that Tom was planning a new life without her.

'So, when do you think you'll be called for an interview?' she asked quietly.

'It could be next week,' he said vaguely. 'Some time after we get back. The interviews will be in London.'

'You said interviews. You mean you'll have to attend more than one interview?'

'What I mean is that they're creating several new posts. It's an expanding company.'

She turned on her side and stared at him across the bed. 'But I thought...'

'Jackie.' He moved slowly across the bed towards her. 'I'm not trying to railroad you, but you have to decide what you're going to do about the Benton merger. The longer you put it off the harder it's going to be. You have to choose between the past and the future.'

'Well, it's obvious that you've chosen where your future lies,' she said icily.

'Yes, I have,' he said, thoughtfully.

He leaned back against his pillows, one hand behind his neck.

'You see, Jackie, when I was with you at the Benton practice I realised that we were surrounded by all the memories of your past. I recognised that there was an almost tangible presence that was keeping you firmly fixed in the past. You've got to make the break, Jackie, otherwise you're always going to be constrained by what happened then.'

He turned towards her and held out his arms. She hesitated. Making love would be so blissful, but at the end of it she would still have to solve her problems. She clasped her hands in front of her, willing herself to remain calm and unemotional.

'Is that why you're leaving Benton?'

'That's one of the reasons. I couldn't bear to think of the unpleasant memories that Benton must evoke for you since Meg told you the full story. I'm sure that now, even though you won't admit it—even to yourself—the bad memories are still with you every time you walk into the surgery. You've got to leave all that behind you and start afresh, Jackie.'

She was silent, her thoughts running through all the years she'd spent at Benton—the good times and the bad. Yes, it was the bad memories that would always be there to haunt her if she stayed. Tom was right.

'If I decide to leave the Benton practice...' she began slowly.

'Oh, darling!'

He was taking her in his arms and this time she didn't resist.

'I didn't dare to hope that you would say that. It had to be your decision. I could see that it was going to take an awful lot of persuasion on my part to influence you. You're such a stubborn, independent woman! But I love you so much! Let's get married, Jackie. Please, please say yes because I know I can't live without you.'

Her heart was pounding rapidly. 'But I thought you were off to start your new life.'

'I can't have a life without you! I've been waiting for you to come to a decision before I tried to persuade you to be part of the plan. I knew I didn't stand a chance unless you made the decision yourself.'

She smiled. The clouds were lifting again. 'So, fill me in on the details of this new venture.'

He paused and took a deep breath. 'Jonathan's company is keen to find a married couple with medical qualifications. You and I would be ideal—we work well together.'

'You mean you're suggesting I should apply for a job with the company as well?'

She stared at him, wide-eyed.

'Only if you want to, Jackie.' He gave her a wry smile. 'As always, it would be your decision.'

'But what about the girls? We can't take them out of school at this stage in their education.'

'They have schools in Paris, you know; in fact, very good schools. And it's obvious that they both love being in France.'

That was true. He was holding her against him, stroking her hair in that sensual way she'd come to love. She loved everything about this man—even the fact that he could twist her round his little finger!

'Would you really have left me if I'd kept the Benton practice going?' she asked quietly.

'No, of course I wouldn't! I'd have stayed on with you and continued to use every trick in the book to persuade you to leave your old life behind. I could see you were in a time warp that was sapping your strength, affecting your health. I had to get you away. In desperation, I thought that if I told you I was going to leave it might spur you into making the decision to move on…into the future—our future together.'

She smiled. 'You can be very persuasive.'

'So, will you marry me, Jackie?'

She heard the husky tone of his voice, saw the tender expression in his eyes and knew that marriage to Tom was the only thing that mattered to her. Everything else would fall into place if only they could be together…always.

'Yes, I'll marry you,' she said quietly.

His arms tightened around her as he kissed her gently on the lips. She could feel the desire rising up inside her, demanding fulfilment.

With a sigh she capitulated, revelling in the tide of sensual passion that was sweeping her along. She moulded her fluid body against his, her hands caressing every beloved, exciting part of him.

And as they clung together their love-making was breath-taking, from the beginning of the first, sensuous caress to the wild, ecstatic, mutual climax at the end.

Afterwards, as she lay back against the pillows with Tom's arm lightly around her, she knew, without a shadow of a doubt, that she'd made the right decision.

She was going forward to a new, exciting life, leaving the past behind. And she also knew that the girls would be so thrilled about it!

During the last few days she'd come to realise what a wonderful relationship Debbie and Fiona now had with Tom. He would never replace their father, but she was sure that he would be the one they would turn to in the future when they needed a father figure.

'We'll have to make plans,' she said, trying to sit up.

Tom's arms pulled her back into a reclining posture. 'Plenty of time for plans,' he said huskily, as he nibbled her ear.

'Yes, but we've got to think about interviews, a wedding, who to invite, where we'll live...'

'Relax, darling.' He raised himself on one elbow. 'The interviews are fixed for next Friday and—'

'Why, you!' She picked up a pillow and aimed it towards his head. 'All this time, you never said a word about it.'

'I was relying on you making your decision. The deadline for cancelling the interviews is tomorrow. I was going to have to use all my powers of persuasion tonight. I would have had to take you in my arms—like this.' She was laughing as he pretended to show her how he would have persuaded her.

'OK, you've convinced me, remember?'

'Better make sure,' he told her as he kissed her hungrily.

Incredibly, she felt her desire rising again in response to his caresses. This was going to be some night...

The sun was peeping over the window-sill when she awoke. Outside she could hear the birds singing in the garden. From downstairs came the sound of laughter and the strong aromatic smell of French coffee.

She rolled over on her side to put her arm over Tom.

'How much do you think we should tell everybody about our plans this morning?' she asked.

He reached out and pulled her against him. 'We should tell them everything. The fact that we're hoping to work together in Paris and that everybody's invited to the wedding in December.'

'December?' she asked. 'Why December?'

'It's my fortieth birthday. We can combine the celebrations—and Christmas.'

'Why not get married in the spring? Easter, perhaps?'

He kissed her gently. 'I can't wait that long for you to make an honest man of me.'

She laughed. 'OK, you win. We'll make it December. Let's go and tell everybody, shall we?'

'Not just yet. There's plenty of time.'

'Did I ever tell you, Tom, that you can be very persuasive?'

EPILOGUE

JACKIE looked out through the sitting room window of their beautiful home on the outskirts of Paris. Set on a small hill, the view of the city was spectacular. They were just far enough away from the hustle and bustle of central Paris for it to feel as peaceful as the countryside, but near enough for Tom to drive to the company clinic in a matter of minutes—depending on the traffic!

Tom poked his head round the door. 'Would you like to come up and tell me what you think about the new painting?'

She smiled. She was glad that, since moving out to Paris a couple of years ago, Tom had still found time to keep up his painting. The hours spent working at the company's clinic were shorter than he'd spent at the practice in England. They had time for leisure pursuits, time for each other—and the children.

The twins, now studying in London—Debbie at medical school and Fiona at drama school—both came home in the holidays and doted on their little brother.

Jackie followed Tom upstairs, pausing on the landing to peep through the half-open door. Baby Timothy was lying on his back, spread-eagled, his covers kicked away. She tip-toed across and tucked a blanket around him. He sighed in his sleep. She touched the soft blond hair and felt a wave of pure happiness sweeping over her.

It had been the right decision to leave her old life behind and begin afresh. She enjoyed every minute of her new life. There were no regrets.

She remembered how she'd returned from their holiday in the château near Bordeaux, her head spinning with all the plans she and Jonathan had to make. She'd been dreading the interview, but it had gone well for both of them. As Jonathan had predicted, the company medical team thought they were ideal for the job.

Helen had been delighted to hear that the Benton surgery was to be merged with Estersea. Although she was sad that Jackie wasn't going with her to Estersea, she was thrilled to hear about the wedding plans. She'd made Jackie promise to keep in touch by fax, phone or letter.

Jackie smiled to herself as she remembered that the latest letter from Helen had said she'd now moved up from medical secretary to deputy practice manager at Estersea. Her organisational skills were being put to full use at last!

Immediately after they'd secured the contract for the Paris job, Jackie had put the cottage and the Benton practice in the hands of an estate agent. Both properties had been snapped up quickly.

Amazingly, the surgery had been turned into a pub! She'd been back once and had hardly recognised the interior with its tables and chairs grouped near the bar, which had been built in the section that had housed the old reception area.

She'd been surprised when Ethel Dunton's son, Bill, had put in an offer for the cottage as soon as it went on the market. Bill had told her he'd been looking for the right property for some time.

It appeared that he wanted to get his mother into a more comfortable home, away from the draughty, inconvenient old farmhouse. He was planning to sell the farm, and also, he'd shyly admitted, he was thinking of getting married to a young widow in the next village. They would all be able to move into the cottage after the wedding.

She'd actually gone back from Paris for Bill's wedding. Mrs Dunton had begged her to be there, saying that she'd always thought of her as the daughter she wished she'd had. The old lady was delighted she'd now got a daughter-in-law and was fervently hoping she could 'hang on long enough' to hear the pitter-patter of tiny feet in the cottage.

Mrs Dunton loved the cottage as much as Jackie loved her home here in Paris.

And they'd been fortunate in being able to buy the other half of Jonathan's château near Bordeaux from the French couple who felt they were now too old to look after two homes. They'd sold it to them at a very reasonable price because they said they wanted it to go to a family who would love it as much as they did.

She now loved the old château as much as the Paris house, especially since that was where they'd held their wedding two years ago in December.

She would never forget that Christmas! The tree in the large hall, all the children singing around it, Tom's mother lending her a valuable diamond necklace from the Prestwick family and saying it was 'something borrowed'—then insisting after the wedding that Jackie kept it. So many happy memories!

As she tucked in the baby's blanket she knew she could never have changed her life for the better without Tom.

He was standing in the doorway, his expressive eyes tender as he watched her with their son. He was holding out his hand. She took it and walked along with him to the room they called his studio.

Jackie always joked that Tom had bagged the best room in the house, but she knew he needed good light for his paintings so she didn't mind them having to sleep in a smaller bedroom. It made it all the more cosy, all the more intimate. So long as there was room for their large, wide, comfy bed she didn't mind where they slept so long as they were together.

She stood back to admire the painting. It was the view from the window—the tall church spires, a glimpse of the

industrial buildings of La Defense and a spidery outline of
the Eiffel Tower in the distance.

'Do you ever miss your little house by the water in
Estersea, Tom?' she asked quietly.

He put his arm around her waist. 'What do you think?'

'Well, I remember how you were searching for a simpler
way of life, and then you took on all of us and—'

'And I've never been happier. How about you? Don't you
sometimes miss being the big white chief in your senior partner room?'

She laughed. 'I never think about it. I enjoyed working in
the company clinic before Timothy was born, but I don't
miss that either. One day I'll take a part-time post but not
until Timothy's well established at school. I don't want to
miss his baby years. They're too precious.'

She started to leave, but he tightened his grip on her waist.
'Don't go.'

'I thought you wanted to paint.'

'I thought so, too, until you came up here. Now I've got
a better idea.'

She laughed. 'The baby's going to wake up. We haven't
time.'

'We've got all the time in the world. We've got the rest
of our lives...'

MAY 1998 HARDBACK TITLES

ROMANCE

In Bed with a Stranger *Lindsay Armstrong*	H4836	0 263 15766 0
Summer Seduction *Daphne Clair*	H4837	0 263 15767 9
Showdown! *Ruth Jean Dale*	H4838	0 263 15768 7
Forbidden Pleasure *Robyn Donald*	H4839	0 263 15769 5
Girl Trouble *Sandra Field*	H4840	0 263 15770 9
A Husband's Price *Diana Hamilton*	H4841	0 263 15771 7
Birthday Bride *Jessica Hart*	H4842	0 263 15772 5
The Twenty-Four-Hour Bride *Day Leclaire*	H4843	0 263 15773 3
Wanted: Perfect Partner *Debbie Macomber*		
	H4844	0 263 15774 1
The Daddy Trap *Leigh Michaels*	H4845	0 263 15775 X
Joined by Marriage *Carole Mortimer*	H4846	0 263 15776 8
Nanny by Chance *Betty Neels*	H4847	0 263 15777 6
The Princess and the Playboy *Valerie Parv*		
	H4848	0 263 15778 4
The Marriage Surrender *Michelle Reid*	H4849	0 263 15779 2
Dante's Twins *Catherine Spencer*	H4850	0 263 15780 6
Gabriel's Mission *Margaret Way*	H4851	0 263 15781 4

HISTORICAL ROMANCE™

Rebecca's Rogue *Paula Marshall*	H431	0 263 15758 X
Dear Deceiver *Mary Nichols*	H432	0 263 15759 8

MEDICAL ROMANCE™

Hero's Legacy *Margaret Barker*	M349	0 263 15756 3
Forsaking All Others *Laura MacDonald*	M350	0 263 15757 1

MILLS & BOON®

MAY 1998 LARGE PRINT TITLES

ROMANCE

Wildcat Wife *Lindsay Armstrong*	1095	0 263 15559 5
The Reluctant Fiancée *Jacqueline Baird*	1096	0 263 15560 9
The Divorcee Said Yes! *Sandra Marton*	1097	0 263 15561 7
Dishonourable Intent *Anne Mather*	1098	0 263 15562 5
The Fortunes of Francesca *Betty Neels*	1099	0 263 15563 3
Marriage on the Rebound *Michelle Reid*	1100	0 263 15564 1
Holding on to Alex *Margaret Way*	1101	0 263 15565 X
The Secret Mother *Lee Wilkinson*	1102	0 263 15566 8

HISTORICAL ROMANCE™

Marrying for Love *Sally Blake*	0 263 15528 5
The Baron's Bride *Joanna Makepeace*	0 263 15529 3

MEDICAL ROMANCE™

Wait and See *Sharon Kendrick*	0 263 15453 X
Too Close for Comfort *Jessica Matthews*	0 263 15454 8
Second Chance *Josie Metcalfe*	0 263 15455 6
Doctor Delicious *Flora Sinclair*	0 263 15456 4

MILLS & BOON®

JUNE 1998 HARDBACK TITLES

MILLS & BOON®

JUNE 1998 LARGE PRINT TITLES

ROMANCE

Up Close and Personal! *Sandra Field*	1103	0 263 15583 8
Bride Required *Alison Fraser*	1104	0 263 15584 6
A Rumoured Engagement *Catherine George*		
	1105	0 263 15585 4
Beauty and the Boss *Lucy Gordon*	1106	0 263 15586 2
Mission: Make-Over *Penny Jordan*	1107	0 263 15587 0
Reluctant Father! *Elizabeth Oldfield*	1108	0 263 15588 9
Just for a Night *Miranda Lee*	1109	0 263 15589 7
A Man Worth Waiting For *Helen Brooks*	1110	0 263 15590 0

HISTORICAL ROMANCE™

A Lord for Miss Larkin *Carola Dunn*	0 263 15457 2
The Impossible Earl *Sarah Westleigh*	0 263 15530 7

MEDICAL ROMANCE™

A Very Special Need *Caroline Anderson*	0 263 15535 8
A Healing Season *Jessica Matthews*	0 263 15536 6
Happy Christmas, Doctor Dear *Elisabeth Scott*	0 263 15537 4
A Father for Christmas *Meredith Webber*	0 263 15538 2